Killing Blue Devils
A Gussie Spilsbury Mystery

Laura Haferkorn

Copyright © 2014 by Laura Haferkorn
First Edition – 2014

ISBN
978-1-4602-4570-5 (Hardcover)
978-1-4602-4571-2 (Paperback)
978-1-4602-4572-9 (eBook)

All rights reserved.

No part of this publication may be reproduced in any form, or by any means, electronic or mechanical, including photocopying, recording, or any information browsing, storage, or retrieval system, without permission in writing from the publisher.

Cover illustration - Sonya Shannon, Artware Studios, Inc.
Author's photograph - Krista Christou

Any resemblance to persons living or dead, or to places and events which appear in this book, are strictly coincidental, and are creations of the author's imagination.

Produced by:

FriesenPress
Suite 300 – 852 Fort Street
Victoria, BC, Canada V8W 1H8

www.friesenpress.com

Distributed to the trade by The Ingram Book Company

DEDICATION

Lovingly dedicated to Canute.
my husband of 60 years,
my best friend, severest critic and staunchest supporter.

And to my four beautiful and talented daughters,
Krista, Sonya, Lisa and Stasia.

ACKNOWLEDGEMENTS

A sincere thank you to Pat Johnston
and to all the people I've met over the years
from city to country to small town
who have generously shared their stories with me.

Table of Contents

1 BACK TO THE LAND? 1
2 HEADING NORTH. BUT WHERE? 7
3 WHAT'S UP WITH SAINT PEEPS? 11
4 WHAT TO DO ABOUT MAC? 17
5 MYSTERY TREK 23
6 DAFFY'S DILEMMA 31
7 JESSE GETS A JOLT 37
8 IS IT JUST GOSSIP OR … 41
9 HUNG OVER! 45
10 PARTY TIME! 49
11 LADY IN BLUE 57
12 WITCHING NEEDED HERE 61
13 SYD STEPS IN 65
14 REVELATION AND RELIEF 69
15 JESSE IS WORRIED 73
16 DOTTIE GETS AN EARFUL 77
17 STRANGE LAKE 81
18 UNANSWERED QUESTION 87
19 RAB KEEPS MUM 89
20 GUSSIE IS SWAMPED 91
21 SYD IS DISAPPOINTED 95

22 DOTTIE ISN'T GIVING UP 99
23 THE BONEYARD 103
24 DOTTIE CONTINUES HER CAMPAIGN 109
25 MONDAY MORNING BLUES 113
26 MORE BAD NEWS 117
27 TOUCH AND GO 119
28 A CURIOSITY 121
29 HEART TO HEART 123
30 2 + 2 = ? 125
31 COLD FEET? 129
32 THE MYSTERY DEEPENS 131
33 A NEW CRIME IN TOWN? 135
34 DING DONG BELL …..................................... 141
35 PLAYING THE WAITING GAME 147
36 FACE OFF 149
37 EMPTY COOP 153
38 QUESTIONS, QUESTIONS 157
39 SHAKE-UP AT SAINT PEEPS 159
40 MR. CUTTLECOMBE TELLS A STORY 163
41 NOT MUCH TO GO ON, BUT … 169
42 KILLING BLUE DEVILS 171
POSTSCRIPT 175

KILLING BLUE DEVILS

Something strange happened here once
A long time ago.
Something strange and terrible.
You can feel it in the air
Especially when the wind blows through the pine trees.
Those ancient trees know what happened.
The story was passed on to them by their great-great-grandparents.
But they'll never tell.
Neither will the grasses.
There are secrets here, waiting to be discovered.
You will have to look under the trees, under the grasses, under the water to find them.
If you dare.

1
BACK TO THE LAND?

Looking back, Dottie Kibbidge called it 'the most thrillin' time in me whole life' and was quick to add, 'but that ole place sure give me the willies!' And to think it all started with something as simple as her brother's sudden urge to own a farm. She couldn't believe so many things could happen that were new to her. And in such a short time. She'd never been inside a police station. Never dreamed of being able to help the police solve a puzzle. Never even been within spitting distance of a really big crime. And a crime that was still a mystery. And all because of the demands the newcomers to East Thorne were making when they came into the little grocery store her brother owned.

Why farming at this stage of his life was beyond her; Rab, whose only harvesting experience had been out on the Grand Banks in their father's boat catching cod.

"What Rab knows 'bout farmin' 'n such ... well, what's it they say 'bout the head of a pin?" Dottie confided to her friend CeeCee Denton one afternoon in mid-April, while they were enjoying a bit of early spring sunshine on the new back porch. CeeCee had just come back from a quick trip into the City to pick up some lamps she'd ordered. She didn't dare have them delivered, they were so fragile. A kind of Tiffany, she told Dottie, who loved bright colours and could hardly wait until they were unpacked.

It seemed to Dottie that CeeCee was always rushing off somewhere. After Hink Denton was found murdered in the woods over by the Old

Barge Canal road, the Kibbidges invited CeeCee to live with them in the village of East Thorne, known locally as East Tee. That had been such a difficult winter for everyone, when the masses of snow from an unpredicted blizzard in late November were still on the ground in March. With intense cold and a ton more snow. No January thaw that year. If young Jesse Woodcock hadn't stumbled over Hink's body and been too frightened to tell Constable Gussie about his discovery, or if Constable Gussie hadn't believed his story, CeeCee would have been left wondering what had happened to him. All winter long. Or longer.

Dottie told CeeCee she should wait a year before making any big decisions. Anyway, that's what she'd heard somewhere. But CeeCee took no time in deciding to sell the big house she and Hink had retired to in the countryside not too far away from the town of Bickerton. CeeCee had chosen her real estate agent well and the house sold for the asking price within a month. She'd been a house guest at the Kibbidges for nearly a year and a half already, but she knew they weren't anxious for her to leave. Good thing too. She was happy there.

"When he tol' me what was weighin' on his mind th'other day as I was gettin' the lunch on, I near dropped th' chowder pot on the floor. Yeah, kinda warm for chowder now," she added before CeeCee could say anything, "but Rab brought home some cod, Lord knows where he got it, needed cookin' up so I decided to make us a batch."

Dottie paused just long enough to take one good swallow of her lemonade. "Turned out pretty good, doncha think, even if the cod was a bit froze." She swirled the ice around in her glass and took another swallow. "When I had a think on it, he's done so good with the store 'n all, I just couldn't give him a good argument why not. Long as the farm isn't a long way aways."

CeeCee had to agree. Rab *had* done well. The little grocery store had grown so much it was almost bursting out of its walls. The more unusual the stock Rab brought in, the more customers he attracted. It wasn't just the location. The area had changed a lot since Rab hopped off the bus that was taking him Out West to try his luck. Like his brothers before him.

For generations, the men in the Kibbidge family had never known anything but fishing and the uncertainty that went along with that existence. Now, with the fish getting scarcer every year, especially the cod they all relied on, they were spreading their wings. So far as Rab knew, none of them had given up and flown back to the home nest.

When Rab got off the bus that day up on the main highway to have a coffee and stretch his legs, he liked what he saw: hundreds of silver birches and pine trees clinging to the hillsides and the valleys between. Neat green fields below. And on the horizon, a sliver of blue water. He let the bus go off without him. When he popped into East Thorne's only store to see where he could pick up some work, Old Elmer Jimson took to him right away. No wonder. Here was a strong young fellow with a ruddy complexion and ready smile that crinkled his soft brown eyes. He looked like he'd be able to tackle anything.

Lately, Elmer had been feeling his strength leaving him and was trying to decide whether to sell out or hang on a bit longer. One look at Rab and his decision was made. Elmer told Rab he was hired on, 'only temp'ry, y'understand,' as a sort of all-round handyman. The young fellow was such a willing worker that it wasn't long before temporary slid into permanent. Several years later when Elmer died, he left the store to Rab, who quickly discovered he had a knack for the business. Besides, his customers loved him. They knew he gave them fair prices and fresh merchandise, along with his personal touch, never mind the times he stayed open late for them when there was bad weather. Or any other kind of crisis.

After that endless snowy winter of nearly two years ago, and the early spring event forever after known as the Big Thaw setting off a near panic in the neighbourhood of East Tee, Rab had rushed all over hell's half acre, as Dottie put it, hauling in extra supplies for his customers who were terrified of being flooded out. Things like kegs of fresh water, and coal oil lamps, and matches in waterproof boxes, and rubber boots. Word quickly got around about Rab's efforts, bringing him in more business than ever.

After his sister Dottie arrived to keep house for him, he added another room to the cramped store. In one corner, he'd put up shelving for Dottie's boxes of yarn and knitting needles and patterns. No one in Bickerton, on the other side of the bridge spanning the Old Barge Canal, was selling craft supplies. Being an avid knitter, Dottie soon met others like herself and figured it was too bad to waste the good of the day running all the way over to Dunhampton for yarns. Besides, Dunhampton was almost a small city. Too many cars. Since coming to Ontario to join her brother, she'd had a hankering to have her own little business. Rab told her okay, but she'll be all your baby, Dot, I don't have time for such things. CeeCee added a few dollars to help get things started. And a few suggestions for promoting the infant enterprise.

CeeCee was a newcomer to the area. And as far as the locals were concerned, she always would be. Although her daughters urged her to move back to the City with them after she was left alone, it was too late. CeeCee had fallen in love with the place and refused to leave. She and Dottie had met at the Bickerton Public Library one day and formed an instant friendship. She'd gratefully accepted the Kibbidges' offer of hospitality. As to staying with them permanently, well, she still hadn't made up her mind. She enjoyed working in the store, restocking the shelves, and helping Dottie with the housework. Except for the cooking. That chore she quite happily left to Dottie, being satisfied to clean up the kitchen and the pots and pans after meals.

After the country house was sold and Hink's estate settled, CeeCee found she had enough money for a little trip Back East. Since the Kibbidges had come into her life, she'd gotten really curious about the part of Canada where they'd grown up. She took Dottie with her and they had a great time visiting Dottie's multitude of friends and relatives in the outports. But after three weeks, Dottie started worrying about leaving Rab on his own so long, so they came back home to get going with the Knittin' Bin, as Dottie called her new venture. Besides, as she put it, if they stayed any longer, they were going to wear out their welcome.

East Thorne was beginning to shape up as a full-blown retirement community. The houses clustered along the tree-lined edges of the Old Barge Canal made lovely escapes for city folk who longed to leave the noise and the crowds behind them, even if only for summer weekends. These houses were huge, built back when the Canal was still used to haul lumber and the area had been at the peak of its prosperity, a situation it wouldn't likely enjoy again. Some houses rose as high as three storeys, with airy attics and wide front porches overlooking the Canal. But most of them were sadly run down. Now city people were discovering them and deciding to retire there. They were fixing up the big old houses and building even bigger ones. No dinky little cottages for them, like those down at The Landing on the Lake.

Arriving in ever greater numbers from the City and its eastern suburbs, Rab's new customers were becoming more and more demanding. Dottie was beginning to think some of them had taken early retirement just so they could spend more time trying out new recipes. Almost daily, it seemed, one of them would be in the shop asking for something Rab had never heard of. Things like Chinese cabbage. And cilantro. And baby potatoes.

"Whatever do you s'pose baby potatoes are? Potatoes for babies? Never heard such nonsense in me life," Rab said one evening, when they were enjoying a Jiggs dinner hastily thrown together by Dottie, who'd been puzzling over order books for yarn all afternoon and had forgotten the time. She loved to collect recipes from her mother's friends Back East. Jiggs was a particular favourite.

"And what's wrong with reg'lar cabbage? Like this here we're eatin'?" Rab went on, helping himself to another good spoonful of the vegetable, along with a thick slice of salt beef.

"Them newcomers got money, though, Rab. Ya gotta agree to that," added Dottie. "CeeCee says that special stuff's not cheap, back where she comes from. Eh, CeeCee?"

CeeCee, who wasn't keen on parsnips and hoped they wouldn't notice she was carefully piling them up on the edge of her plate, put down her fork. She remembered Hink coming home one night and talking about some new little shop near his office where they sold unusual fruit and vegetables out front. Chinese mostly, he thought. At least the owner who stood out on the street chatting up passers-by sounded Chinese to him.

"No, it isn't. But where you'd get it from way out here is beyond me," she said slathering more mustard on her plate, burying the hated parsnips. "Even mustard, now. Comes in umpteen different kinds. Hink always favoured the French stuff. To me, mustard is mustard. But he had to have a bottle of Dee John on the dinner table. Or nothing. Even that comes in coarse or fine."

Brother and sister exchanged looks. It had been months since CeeCee had spoken Hink's name. In the time since the murder, and the trial that attracted so much attention from the newspapers, even the dailies in the City, they'd avoided any subject that might come close to stirring up the feelings of their guest. It was hard to think of her as a guest, as it seemed as if she'd always been with them, she'd fit into their little family so easily.

The meal continued in silence, Dottie trying to think up a suitable response to CeeCee's comments, and CeeCee wondering what on earth had made her think of Hink now. It was odd she hadn't spent much time mourning his loss. She guessed it was because he had been so controlling, something she'd put up with over their long years of marriage without realizing it. Now her newfound freedom kept her so busy she hadn't thought too much about her former life.

Rab, who never had much to say at any time, methodically cleaned his plate with a heel of Dottie's brown bread, wiped his fingers on his napkin and folded it neatly in two. Abruptly, he pushed his chair back from the table and said, "Well, what's wrong with tryin' to grow that fancy stuff meself?"

The two women looked at him in surprise. Before they could say a word, Rab excused himself and went out the door that led to the store. Almost immediately he was back, looking sheepish.

"Some good dinner that was. Forgot to thank you, Dot."

He was gone again, leaving Dottie sitting there, still speechless. She couldn't remember a time when Rab had thanked her for anything.

2
HEADING NORTH. BUT WHERE?

"Better put that pup down before you drop him!" Kitty admonished, as Jesse shot into the kitchen, his arms full of curly black fur. Two bright eyes peered through a shaggy fringe at Kitty, while a feathery tail beat a steady rhythm on Jesse's side. Breathless boy and bundle of fur dropped onto one of the kitchen chairs, dark hair mingling, as Jesse, whose own thick black curls hung low over his forehead, buried his face in the pup's neck.

"You're going to spoil him if you keep that up," Kitty went on, as she put a plate of freshly baked muffins on the table to cool, trying not to let her son see how pleased she was to see him so happy. Wiping her hands on her apron, she flipped her long braid of yellow hair back over her shoulder. "And where's the fire anyways?"

For more than a year now, Jesse's personality had been undergoing a transformation from happy-go-lucky little boy to moody adolescent. No more staying at the table after supper, cheerfully relating the day's events. No more working at his crossword puzzles, while Kitty did the supper dishes, Jesse asking her every few minutes if she knew how to spell a certain word. And when he came home from school, he went straight upstairs and disappeared into his room, doing Heaven knows what for hours, and had to be called down for his meals. He'd always been a companionable sort of kid and Kitty missed his lively presence. His parents put it down to the frightening afternoon when he'd stumbled over the lifeless body of Hink Denton in the woods. His father, Albie, had been away on a secret assignment to do with his government job which meant he hadn't been around when it happened. And his mother, Kitty, who lived through it with Jesse, was still feeling guilty she hadn't been able to deal with the situation the way she figured a good mother was supposed to do.

The Woodcocks were glad their son was doing better in school now that Lettice Snelgrove was gone. He was delighted with his new teacher, Sherry Roxton, Bickerton's former librarian, who had decided to revive her teaching certificate and tackle the Grade Eights at the Junior School. She was just as crazy about birds as Jesse and had started up a little Nature Club, where Jesse with all his birding knowledge was the star. Jesse had always been full of fun, energetic, a regular 'ball of fire', his mother told everyone she met. But finding the body had changed him somehow. Since that time, he'd never ventured into the woods alone. Death had become a stark reality, and he looked at life more seriously than he had before.

The arrival of the pup, a present from a grateful CeeCee Denton, had given him a new sense of responsibility, along with the companion he so sorely needed. His best friend, Adam Brant, was gone. Where, not even Adam's own parents knew. Last summer, a travelling carnival had lumbered into town and when it moved on, from something Adam had said earlier made Jesse suspect his friend had left with it. But the Brants hadn't given up. They were still hoping their wayward son would get in touch with them. So far, nothing but silence.

Setting the pup down on the floor, Jesse stood up and took a deep breath. "Mister Rab, well, um, he 'n Miz Denton 'n Miz Kibbidge, um, they're goin' up to, well, I'm not too sure where they're goin', I think somewheres up past the Lonesome River. Mister Rab he's, um, lookin' at somethin' up there, Miz Denton said, 'n they want me to go with 'em, Mister Rab's got this real neat big box on the back of his truck, can I go with 'em, can I, Mom, can I?"

"It's *may* I," said Kitty resignedly. "Don't they teach you anything at that school?"

"Okay, then *may* I go with 'em? It's only for a little while 'n Pop said he'd be back real early, so's we can get ready to go fishin' tomorrow," Jesse said, grabbing a still-warm muffin and popping it into his mouth. He reached over for another one which disappeared into his back pocket. It was a sunny Saturday afternoon and Jesse had spent most of the morning out in the yard playing with the pup.

"I guess it's all right, seeing as how you've done your chores for today. You *have* done them, haven't you, son?" Kitty moved to check under the sink to see if the garbage had been emptied. It had, so she straightened up again, feeling a bit stiff. Her cheeks were flushed from having spent the morning scrubbing down the basement floor, which hadn't seen soap and water since she couldn't remember when. An unusually warm spring day was a good time to be down in the cool of the basement. Albie was thinking of putting in a model railroad down there for Jesse. A friend had given him some cars and an engine to start off with. Now all he needed to do was put up a high table and lay down some tracks.

"Yup, um, I mean, yes ma'am, all done, got 'em done right after breakfast when you were downstairs." Jesse leaned over to pick up the pup who was trying out his new teeth on the chair leg. Good thing his mom hadn't noticed. She hadn't been too keen on him having a dog. Too much mess in the house. But Jesse made sure to clean up after the pup before she could complain. He was pretty sure the task of housebreaking would soon be finished.

"Well then, off you go. When are they coming to get you?" Kitty asked, wiping her hands on her apron.

"They're here now!"

"Here? Outside, you mean?"

Jesse nodded, slinging the pup over his shoulder.

"Oh for goodness sakes, why didn't you say so?" Kitty said. *Wasn't that just like a kid.* "Better get a move on, then. Tell them you have to be home in time for supper, hear?"

But Jesse was gone, out the door as quickly as he'd come in, the pup's head bobbing up and down as if it were on springs.

Kitty ran out after them. "Better take a leash," she called, waving to the occupants of the familiar beat-up old truck with the cab extension waiting at the curb. They waved back. Too late. Jesse had already clambered into the back and the truck moved off.

She turned and went back into the house. Hallelujah! She had the house to herself. For a little while, anyways. Good thing she'd put her foot down when CeeCee Denton had shown up with two puppies. One was plenty, she'd insisted. But CeeCee said she'd brought two so Jesse could choose. One was white with one black ear giving its little face a lopsided look. But Jesse went right for the black one which was smaller and stretched out its neck to sniff his hand. He'd always liked Adam's black dog and besides, this one matched him better, he said. Kitty was glad. White dogs are so much harder to keep looking clean than black ones.

Slowly she went up the stairs to the room she shared with Albie. The bed looked so inviting, she lowered herself carefully onto its welcoming surface, pulling the edge of the quilt over her. She was totally exhausted and it was still early afternoon. Was she getting old or was she just tired from all the floor scrubbing? Lately it seemed to her that everything was taking twice as long as it used to. Maybe she'd better go and see that nice Dr. Blair next week and … she was asleep before she could finish the thought.

She was still there when Albie came home.

3
WHAT'S UP WITH SAINT PEEPS?

Syd Spilsbury was not a happy man. For months now, he'd been trying to unload that part of his life he'd hated for so long. He'd inherited the *Bickerton Bugler*, the town's weekly newspaper, from his father, whose father before him had gotten the whole enterprise off the ground in the first place. His dad had loved the paper and assured Syd he would too. Especially the power he'd wield in the town. You'll have a captive audience, son, he remembered his dad saying more than once. No one else bothers to give the place a mention. We're beneath their notice. Well, that might have been true in his father's day. But, after the sensation created by the Denton murder and the shocking revelations in a 'town full of crooks and criminals' as their larger neighbour Dunhampton's *Daily Doings* had put it, people had come to expect more of the *Bugler's* editor than he was able to give them. And, although Bickerton was growing, not too much had been happening lately in the way of scandals that would satisfy his readers' newly minted craving for the lurid stuff.

He blamed the often unbearable pressure he was under with the *Bugler* for his break-up with Gussie. If it hadn't been for that, he might have been able to put up with her unfortunate habit of repeating herself. That was her father's fault. Mac had stopped her so often when she was still a child and made a mistake in grammar that she was constantly making sure what she said was understood. Syd hadn't been able to stand listening to her and they'd decided to call it quits. Now, with the chance their revived romance might lead to remarriage, he was determined to find another way of making a living. Having two of them in demanding jobs hadn't worked the first time, had it? Better cede that field to Gussie, whose job as Town Constable was keeping her busier than ever. Bickerton was attracting quite a few refugees from the Big Smoke, the locals' name for Toronto. Refugees. Known elsewhere as early retirees.

The City lay an ever shorter distance to the west of them if you took the Four Oh One. Which just about everybody did if they had occasion to go there. When they did, it was usually to one of the larger hospitals to get treatments the hospital in Dunhampton couldn't provide. And when they came home, they told everyone how puzzled they were as to why anyone would want to live there. Too crowded. Too noisy. Too many strange faces. They had to admit they'd been well taken care of by the doctors and nurses. But as for living there, or even shopping, well, who could afford it?

Sitting in his dingy and untidy office on a Friday afternoon, Syd's thoughts refused to move past Gussie. Even after her success in wrapping up the Denton murder case, she'd had no luck in persuading the Town Council to increase their policing budget and hire a deputy. The young lady cop had the perfect candidate in mind. The reliable Perce from up at Cooley's Mills had slogged with her through the long miserable winter months surrounding the Denton case. He worked full time at the mill, but had shown a lot of interest in becoming a policeman. He'd have to go through the training, of course. But Gussie said she didn't know if she could wait that long. She needed someone *now*.

After the uproar around the murder of Hink Denton calmed down, Gussie managed to wangle a new cruiser out of those penny-pinchers on Council. Well, almost new. Dunhampton, where the higher-ups operated, had parted with one of their supercharged Champion Chasers, though they couldn't see how a backwater like Bickerton would ever need a vehicle as powerful as the ChooChoo. Not enough banks worth robbing. Nor homes either. But Gussie told Syd she knew better. Those refugees weren't exactly poverty stricken, were they? Not when you heard from the guys down at the lumber store or the hardware store what they were putting into their houses. Especially into those Victorian antiques in East Tee over by the Old Barge Canal.

Gussie had her problems, all right. But it went farther than that for Syd. He was tired of being tied to the newspaper for what seemed like twenty-four hours a day. Tired of chasing around town to report on local events that bored him silly. Tired of fielding phone calls from irate readers if he didn't make it to some dull meeting. Or if he forgot someone's birthday. Or dared to spell someone's name wrong. Everyone knew everyone else and expected all their important events to be known in detail. They didn't see the need to call and remind their overworked editor before the paper came out. He should have known it automatically, they said. Sure, he had lists and back copies, but he didn't have time to check for every last anniversary, did he? Why couldn't they see that?

Trying to get his mind back on the job, he hunched over the desk, struggling with the wording for a notice announcing a special meeting at Sts. Peter and Paul Union Church, known locally as Saint Peeps. The sheet of paper in front of him that he'd found loose in the mailbox that morning just said 'Thursday night', 'discussion', 'urgent'. No other details. He was doodling a row of question marks when the phone rang. It was Daffy Sturgeon, the church secretary, asking did he get her message and was the notice ready yet and could she see it before it went into the paper? When he hesitated, trying to think of a diplomatic way to ask her what in heck was going on over there, she jumped into the gap.

"Syd, you've got to get that thing done and right away! We've got a serious situation here! Action has to be taken! Coming over in five minutes!" and the phone went dead.

He sat for a moment, still holding the phone and staring at it as if it had bitten him. What serious situation? What action? What on earth was wrong at the church, the last place you'd suspect of having a problem? And hadn't he heard, just last week, that the minister was off fly-fishing somewhere? How could action be taken in his absence?

Until now, Syd had always thought of the church as the one fixed institution in the town. He wasn't a regular member there, but like so many others, he and Gussie had gotten married at good old Saint Peeps. Most people had their babies baptized there. The last stop on life's journey for many of the townsfolk would be a reserved plot in the ancient cemetery that stretched out behind the church as far as the woods bordering the town. The church building might be old, with an uncertain heating system, which meant you got used to leaving your coat on in the wintertime. But it was central to the most important times in many Bickertonians' lives.

They'd gone through a long spell of being without someone to take Daffy's father's place. Old Preach, as he was affectionately called, had been the serving pastor for so long that when he suddenly died, must be all of a year and a half ago now, and in the middle of one of his longwinded sermons, the whole congregation had been thrown into a state of confusion. They'd had to bring in a temporary pastor for weddings and funerals. And ask a couple of members to organize the Sunday services. But Syd thought all that had been taken care of just before last Christmas. He'd covered the first service of the incoming minister and found him to be a little strange on first meeting, but put that down to newcomer's nerves.

After Daffy had been and gone, Syd was no wiser. When he'd gently prodded her to tell him more, she dropped hints that the urgent change involved the new minister. But just exactly what needed changing, she refused to say.

"Just get the notice in the paper this week! People will come out! They'll be dying of curiosity! You'll see! Be there will you?"

With the sound of the door slamming shut behind Daffy still ringing in his ears, he tried again to settle down to work. In vain. His mind kept jumping back to Gussie and the need to get rid of the millstone *Bugler* that was getting heavier by the week. He'd run several ads in other newspapers, even as far away as the City. So far, no nibbles.

Small but growing town on the shores of Lake Monogonquin has weekly newspaper looking for an owner. Excellent circulation extending well beyond town limits. Figures on request. Etc etc etc. All the usual bumf. Maybe it needed jazzing up. *Beautiful area with great fishing? Unlimited boating? Superb hiking?* He'd have to spend more time on the thing.

At this point, he wasn't sure if he wanted it broadcast all over town that the paper was up for sale. The town would be shocked, of course. Why would he want to give up a sure thing? Especially after he'd won Honourable Mention for his piece on the Denton murder? Not many small town newspaper editors ever get that kind of recognition.

That no one in town appeared to have seen the ad in the City papers was amazing. Some people read those papers, he knew that for a fact. He'd seen them from time to time in the barber shop. People always looked embarrassed if he caught them reading anything besides the *Bugler*. Silly, but there it was.

In a town the size of Bickerton, gossip ran through the place like a wind-driven forest fire. Look what happened to poor old Mac Noble, Gussie's father, and one of the principals in the Denton murder scandal. Mac had been lucky. His sentence for conspiracy in the murder plot had been reduced because of ill health. It wouldn't be too long before he'd be coming back to the town where he'd once been mayor. And a popular one at that. But a town where now people frowned or looked away whenever his name was mentioned.

Syd wondered how Gussie managed to carry on after learning her dearest father had known, all those dreadful weeks of the worst winter on record, had known exactly what happened to Hink Denton. Mac had let her go on working her heart out. And her hoping she could solve the case without help from the higher-ups over in Dunhampton. If it hadn't been for Mac's heart attack and what happened after that, she might have had to give up. Oh well. That awful time was behind them now. *Time to move on.*

The last time Syd and Gussie trekked up to the prison at Wildwood to visit Mac, they'd been concerned at the change in him. He'd always been a strong and healthy outdoorsy kind of guy. The whole time they'd been there, with the silent figure of a guard hovering within earshot, Mac sat stolidly on his side of the divide, responding to their questions with grim silence. It was obvious he found their visit awkward. And wasn't particularly happy to see them. On the way back, Gussie said he'd seemed smaller to her somehow. He hadn't been eating much from the look of it, had even lost a tooth. He didn't know what to say when she gave way to tears and cried all the way home. He'd just put his arm around her as she huddled beside him in the old truck.

Since their renewed closeness, which had come about over the Denton case, Syd had replaced their wedding photo on his desk. He picked it up now to admire how full of promise they'd looked back then. Gussie hadn't lost her stunning looks and hadn't aged a bit. In his eyes, anyway. Her long and shiny dark auburn hair had been skilfully wound into a coronet by Maybelle, the local hairdresser, and her flawless complexion was enhanced by the creamy petal-pink of her floor length satin dress. Her mother had been married in that same dress. Mac had saved it all these years for his only daughter's wedding day. Looking more closely at his own image, it was obvious to him that *he'd* aged. Sure, his eyes were as alert as ever, but he'd put on a few pounds since then. Probably eating all the wrong food since they'd separated. And wasn't his hairline starting to recede? It was high time he got out of the pressure cooker the *Bugler* had become.

Through the dusty window across from his desk, he could see the weather was still holding, in spite of a threatened thunderstorm. He planned to take Gussie out for a late dinner. That is, if no emergencies cropped up between now and 8 p.m. This was as early as she could get away on a Friday night. Not like Saturdays, when there were liable to be fights to be broken up, or drunks to be hauled in to dry out. And it was the beginning of the tourist season, and the extra problems that came with the yearly foreigner invasion, as Mac used to call it. Sighing, which he realized he'd been doing a lot of lately, he got down to finishing the ad for the mysterious emergency meeting at St. Peeps.

4
WHAT TO DO ABOUT MAC?

While Syd was struggling with the ad for the church meeting, Gussie was trying to catch up on some paperwork. In spite of the long working hours and the large area she had to cover, she'd decided long ago she really loved her job. Not being tied to a desk was the best part, but sometimes she thought she didn't spend enough time there. The never-ending paperwork demanded her attention. Too much of it, she often felt.

Most Bickertonians were law-abiding. Gussie thought the old saying about rolling up the sidewalks at night could well apply to Bickerton. Saturday night was still the biggest night in town, when the stores stayed open later and the farmers from the surrounding countryside brought their families in to shop and socialize. Sure, some of the young men could be rowdy at times, but usually they were just letting off steam after a tough week in the fields or in the factories. There always seemed to be one or two troublemakers. The others usually managed to keep the lid on and distract them before they could get into really serious trouble.

Her main worry now was her father. She knew she must not, under any circumstances, let it interfere with her job. But try as she might, she couldn't rid herself of the thought that she should have seen what was going on with him. It had taken her a long time to accept the fact that her own beloved dad had been part of the group who conspired to get rid of Hink Denton. *I can't believe he didn't stop them before it went too far,* kept running through her head, especially in the early hours of the morning. *He must have known it was wrong, that it would cause me a lot of work to sort out. And this was the man who was so encouraging when I wanted to make law enforcement my career.* But this kind of thinking was a waste of her time. Her father, MacPherson Noble, was as guilty as the rest of them. She hoped he was aware of just how steep a price he was paying for his lapse in judgment, watching his formerly excellent health deteriorate. Knowing the whole town where he'd lived and worked for so many years would certainly shun him when he finally came back home. Or should that be if, not when?

Whenever she could find a couple of hours, Gussie made an effort to put some kind of order into his belongings. And to clean his house, even though she knew it wasn't likely he'd be able to live in it any more. After Mac's arrest, she and Syd went down to the old house by the Lake one Sunday afternoon with no idea of how much there was to do. They'd been amazed at how much junk was stored in the basement. Acres of cartons piled to the ceiling. Stacks of old magazines and newspapers. They could see Mac was one of those people who can't bear to throw anything away. Typical of someone brought up with the cloud of the Great Depression hanging over his head. Or so they reasoned.

The few times she'd been able to drop in on Mac, the place looked clean enough. But when she got down to it, she realized he'd been careful to keep the living room picked up and dusted. He'd even managed to run the old-fashioned sweeper over the worn carpets and swabbed down the kitchen linoleum. She hadn't noticed the dirt lurking in the corners. The sweeper had never done much of a job, but Mac refused to have an electric vacuum cleaner. Said they were too noisy.

After Buff, his old retriever died, he didn't want another dog. Made too much mess, he said, rolling on the carpets, leaving hairs everywhere, dirty paw marks on the kitchen floor. He'd explained all this to Gussie when she told him he needed a dog. For company, if nothing else. It bothered her that he was all alone in the old place. But Mac said he was used to it and wouldn't consider, even for five minutes, moving into town. They'll have to carry me out of this place feet first, girl, he'd always said when the subject came up. But now, living out his last days in his own home didn't seem possible.

"When you get right down to it, the place is worse than a pigsty, I mean, a pigsty," Gussie had stated firmly, that first day when they'd had a chance to check the house over. "Something has to be done."

Syd had to agree. He hated to see her take on anything else at this point and managed to get her to admit she was working hard enough now. But his mind was not on what to do with the house. He had his own problems, deciding what to do with the *Bugler*. Maybe when that problem was solved, he would be able to concentrate on doing something else for a change.

"How did your dad manage, living on his own like he did?" the new doctor asked Gussie, one freezing cold day not long after the trial, when he'd come into the police station, for what she couldn't remember.

"Oh, he does, I mean, he did. Okay. I mean, okay. Yes. He did. Okay." She pretended to concentrate on some papers to do with a case. She really didn't want to discuss it. Especially with the doctor she thought was a bit too nosey. In vain she tried to smother the guilt that insisted on surfacing when anyone mentioned her father. Since she'd taken on the job of policing the area, she'd been so busy, she really didn't have a clue how he'd managed. In the old days, when he wanted to see her, Mac would come up to town and they'd try to get out for a quick lunch. Or a coffee. She rarely had time for him on weekends. Domestic problems cropped up most often when the men were off work. Or vandalism by the kids whose parents didn't have time for them. Or accidents from the extra traffic up on the Highway. And in between? Paperwork. There was always that eternal mountain of paperwork that had to be conquered.

"Can you get someone to go in and clean for him? His heart will never be up to heavy work again, you know. And how is he in the cooking department?" Dr. Blair persisted. "Hey, the restaurants in this burg are no heck, are they? And that awful greasy spoon down at The Landing, well, I guess it's closed now, but …"

"Yeah, the Cosy Corner is about it here in town all right. It's okay for a light lunch or even a proper breakfast once in a while, I mean, once in a while." *Why doesn't he leave? He's just angling for a date and the answer is still no.* Aloud she said, "The food hasn't been the same there since Jennie Brant left." The doctor nodded in agreement.

Gussie put down one sheaf of papers and picked up another, wishing the doctor would take the hint. "Dad fixed his own breakfast, that is, on days when he got up early enough to eat it. Most mornings he slept late. He says it's much worse now, I mean, much worse. Not being able to get to sleep. But I figured it was being in that zoo of a prison, with strange noises all night." She shuddered, knowing in her heart of hearts Mac was suffering from that greatest of all insomnia-makers – a guilty conscience.

"He told me he had the same trouble when Mom was still alive," she went on. "Old Doc Winter wanted to give him something, but he said nothing doing, I mean, nothing doing. While he was telling me, he got real mad at Old Doc, I mean, real mad. All over again. His face got real red and he started shouting. Seems he thought Doc was insulting him, putting him on pills like some pantywaist. Whatever that is. At least that's what he said." *Doesn't this guy have anything better to do today but come in here and give me the third degree?* The smarmy look she'd seen on his face told her he was sure she'd fall in with his plans and go out with him. She shifted her chair closer to her desk and bent over the papers in front of her.

The doctor continued to linger in the doorway. "Wonder why no one has seen fit to open a really good restaurant here? We'll have to go out of town somewhere to find a decent meal."

Gussie went on studying the papers, trying hard not to look up. *Not with me you don't.* Aloud she said, "I can tell you why. It's real easy, I mean, real easy. No money in it. This is a farming community, remember? And farmers don't like to eat out, I mean, eat out. Oh, they'll try out a new place. Once. Just so they can say they've been there." She stood up and moved around to the front of her desk. "Why should they eat in a restaurant when they can grow their own food? At least, that's the way they think. And their wives are pretty good cooks, I mean, pretty good cooks. The only time farmers like to eat out that I know of is at church suppers."

Time to get serious. She got up and went over to the doorway. "Now, if you don't mind, I've got work to do, I mean, work to do," she said as sternly as she could. Looking straight at him, she couldn't help noticing how cold his blue eyes were. Cold as ice. Nothing like Syd's warm ones. Easily as tall as he was, she stood her ground, gripping the door knob. When he saw she was serious, the doctor took a step backwards before she could close the door in his face.

Gussie went back to the papers on her desk. It was obvious the darkly handsome Dr. Bill Blair hadn't given up trying to make an impression on her. *Why on earth did I let myself go rambling on? And to the doctor of all people, who thinks he's God's gift to women. Making out like he had real concern for his patient. What a sneaky way to ... oh stop it, Augusta! Why do you always suspect people of having ulterior motives? Is this what happens when you have the mind of a cop?* When she had a chance to think about it later on, it was really her fault. She should have discouraged him ages ago.

She had no intention of getting involved with anyone. She was still confused over her renewed feelings for Syd, who'd dropped a few hints he wanted them to try again. She knew she'd have to do something about their situation. But she couldn't stop thinking about Mac even though he still had a long time to serve out his sentence. What if she sent him up to his sister Meghan's place in North Bay? No. That wouldn't work at all. Not even for a short time. He'd never gotten along with that sister too well. And Meggie was the only one left in his immediate family. Too bad they were both so stubborn and set in their ways. And it was a cinch he couldn't live with *her*. Her tiny apartment was far too small for the two of them. Impossible.

Maybe she should try to persuade him to sell the house. He could certainly use the money. After going through his financial papers, she'd discovered he hadn't been exactly thrifty. She found all kinds of receipts for donations he'd made to causes in and around the town, eating away into his capital. And, if by any chance she and Syd should try living together again, having Mac with them would be an additional strain. He'd be expecting them to come home every night for dinner. As if they had regular jobs. They'd need a bigger place too. No. He'd have to live somewhere else.

After her split with Syd, Gussie had had a hard time finding a decent sized apartment not too far away from the police station. Finally she'd settled for a tiny one bedroom over the pharmacy. Syd's dad's house, which he had inherited, and where he was still living, was not roomy enough for three adults. And anyway, the house would go with the newspaper business when it was sold. So that wouldn't work either. Gussie knew that if she and Syd were going to make it they'd need their privacy. And space.

And then there was another problem. She had too much to do. The town was growing at an unexpected rate, with more newcomers arriving from the City. And arriving in droves in East Tee that was also her responsibility. If only the Town Council could see she needed a deputy. Too bad she'd shown such dedication to the job from the beginning. They thought she could handle anything. Well, she wasn't handling her personal life very well, was she?

5
MYSTERY TREK

"For pity's sakes, where're we headed, Rab? What kinda wild goose chase ya takin' us on anyways? I'm startin' in to feel a bit queasy." Dottie's voice came out in a series of jerks as they bumped along the narrow track. She was sorry she'd given up the space next to the door to CeeCee, with the three of them crammed into the only seat. The trees were pressing in so closely that their branches were scraping along the sides of the truck. The paintwork was sure taking an awful beating. Good thing it was the old rattletrap for hauling firewood Rab had gotten in some kind of a trade with his friend down by the Canal.

They had been underway for nearly an hour now, and after so many twists and turns, if you'd asked her, CeeCee would have had to admit she was totally disoriented. She loved mysterious drives. You never knew what surprises lay at their finish. Hink would never have done anything as harebrained as this. But maybe it wasn't so harebrained. All along she'd been aware Rab was driving with a purpose, so the road was obviously familiar to him. CeeCee thought he'd said something about up Lonesome River way. That was where that nice young Constable Gussie Spilsbury said she and Syd used to go courting. But they must be long past the river now. For all she knew they could have been going in the opposite direction, she felt so turned around.

"Jus' a little farther, girls, not too long now," Rab said without taking his eyes off the track as it meandered through the woods.

In the back of the truck, Jesse was sorry he'd eaten that second muffin. He was feeling a bit seasick or what he imagined seasickness might feel like. He wondered if it happened to dogs too. But the pup was sound asleep on his lap, not all bothered by the bouncing and jouncing. Good thing his mom wasn't with them. She'd have told Mister Kibbidge to turn around, right now, and go back. But there was no place Jesse could see where you could turn a truck around. Or even a small car. No breaks in the wall of trees. Or up ahead either, as far as he could make out, squinting through the tiny window in the cab. He couldn't even talk to the three up in the front.

Just when he thought he couldn't stand it for another minute, the truck came to an abrupt stop, the rear end skidding sideways and jerking the pup awake.

"It's okay now, Buzzy," Jesse whispered, running a finger over the pup's furry head. "Guess we're finally there."

The pup yawned contentedly, showing his pink tongue, and closed his eyes again. Jesse heard the others struggling to climb out and then came a sharp rap on the side of the truck, waking the pup again, who thought it was time he tried out his newly discovered bark.

"All out, young fella, we gotta walk the rest," he heard Mister Kibbidge say, followed by cries of dismay from the two women.

Jesse took a firm grip on the pup and slid out of the truck. It looked like it was going to be a fine spring day. The sun was shining stronger now and a breeze had come up. This might turn out to be fun.

"Didn't say anything about walking, Rab," said CeeCee, who was trying to figure out which way was north. She squinted up at the bright sunlight and rubbed her eyes, which were already watering.

"Not to worry," Rab replied, hauling a stained canvas bag out from under his seat and slamming his door shut. "I already bin up here and cleared a path through. Follow me," and he forged ahead of the truck, along a trail edged by fallen trees. A flock of small birds, waxwings Jesse informed them, flew noisily up into the trees that so far had escaped Rab's axe.

"Gotta watch out for bees. Lots of 'em buzzin' round when I was in before," Rab called back knowing how his sister hated insects of any kind.

Dottie stopped in her tracks. She cut a comical figure in an old pair of Rab's pants and a frayed sweater which was too large for her. A long flannel shirttail hung down under the sweater. "I'm not takin' another step, Rab Kibbidge, 'til ya tells me where all we're headed."

"Come on, Dottie girl," her brother retorted, not missing a step as he slipped his arms through the loops of the canvas bag and hoisted it onto his back. "Can't you never tell when I'm teasin'? Tisn't that far 'long here. But up aways there's a little crick runs acrost so we couldn't bring the truck. It'll be fine, I tell you. Nice day for a hike."

Dottie and CeeCee looked at each other resignedly. Before they could move on, Jesse had passed them and was hurrying to catch up with Rab. He was still carrying the pup, so the little guy wouldn't get lost in the jungle of fallen trees.

Ten minutes or so later, when the women were beginning to think they were going to the ends of the earth, they came to the creek Rab had mentioned. A makeshift bridge of old boards had to be negotiated before they could continue. Dottie scrambled across, but CeeCee paused to look down on the water moving sluggishly beneath her. It was the colour of strong tea and didn't look to be too deep. Small black beetles skittered around in the reeds growing along the banks. She wondered if the creek connected with the Lonesome River.

A little farther along, the path suddenly opened out. Between trees weighed down with wild cucumber vines, CeeCee could see flashes of bright green.

"Sorry, didn't get all this stuff down. It started in to rain so I hadda quit," Rab was waiting for them. "We kin get by through here."

He pushed his way into the tangle of vines and disappeared, with Jesse following close behind. The two women plunged after them and found themselves standing on the edge of an open field. The uneven ground was strewn with rocks. Dark clumps of last summer's weeds dotted the fresh new green of the grasses that were springing up everywhere. The remains of a split rail fence sprawled along one edge. Masses of vines looped up and over what rails were left, most of the posts having long since rotted away.

"Let's keep agoin' now," Rab looked back over his shoulder to see if the women were following. "We're not there yet."

He led the way across the field, skirting the rocks and avoiding the holes that peppered the landscape. The others followed in single file, Dottie not daring to ask again how much farther it might be, and CeeCee hoping those holes weren't full of snakes. Jesse was wishing he'd brought a leash for the pup. He didn't dare put the little guy down in case he fell into one of the holes. The pup was whining now and struggling in his arms.

As Rab seemed to be heading for the far side of the field, the others scrambled to keep up with him. Now they could see a gap in the row of bushes that might have served as a fence. Beyond the opening, a dilapidated structure came into view. And beyond it loomed a larger one. As they got closer, CeeCee could see that nearly half the roof of the smaller building was gone. Closer still, and she spotted a row of roosts through the open doorway. *Aha,* she said to herself, *an old hen house.* As they passed by, the rank smell of mouldy chicken droppings rose up to greet them. CeeCee wrinkled her nose and sneezed, but kept going.

Away off to her right up a slight rise were the remains of a barn. It must have been a fair size, judging from the fieldstone foundation, with its ragged edges making it look like some medieval battlement. The gangway leading up to what would have been the main level was still there, packed along the sides with more stones, some of which had fallen out, leaving gaps like missing teeth.

As she continued picking her way carefully along the rough path, CeeCee began feeling a little strange. Light-headed almost. Puzzling over what might be causing it, she realized what was really bothering her was a growing unease. Something about this place must be to blame. Was she the only one sensing this? She'd often had feelings like this before and had once or twice been startled when she found out later she had good reason to feel uneasy. The worst time was when she'd been visiting a new friend in a house in the oldest part of the City, where the dread that swept over her made her get out of the place in a hurry. She later learned that, years before, a woman had been brutally murdered in an upstairs bedroom. Her killer was never caught.

For a moment, she considered turning back and waiting for the others in the truck. But only for a moment. How could she explain why without them thinking she was crazy? No. She would have to carry on. Making a serious attempt to get back into the pleasant frame of mind she'd been in when they'd started this adventure, she asked herself what on earth could be wrong with an old abandoned farm?

Up ahead, the larger building proved to be what was left of a house of a style common in Southern Ontario – a storey-and-a-half, with a sharp peak over the entrance. So weatherbeaten, like nothing she ever remembered seeing before, it was hard to say what its roof might have been made of, buried as it was under a heavy coat of grayish green lichen.

"Bet that ole place never seen a lick a paint," suggested Dottie, who had paused for breath. "Or if it had, there's sure none of it left." She told CeeCee it reminded her of some of the old houses Back East. Its wooden walls were a smoky gray fading to tarnished silver where many years of strong sunlight had bleached them. The windows on the bottom floor were blanked out with odd pieces of wood, while the top half of the small window over the front door sported a frayed piece of what had once been a curtain. The bottom half was open to the elements.

CeeCee stood and stared at the house in amazement. What in heaven's name was keeping it up? The shape it was in, it should have fallen in years ago. Dottie, who was suffering from the long walk, looked around in vain for a place to sit down. She complained her poor feet were swollen and aching.

"Whadya s'pose Rab is up to now?" she asked CeeCee, "Phew! I'm too hot an' tired to ask him." She took off her sweater and tied it around her ample waist.

Jesse had already disappeared around the house. As they were standing there, they heard him calling them to come quick. As they made their way through the forest of weeds, CeeCee noticed what was left of the front door was dangling by one hinge with only a splintery board barring the way in. All she could make out in the gloom was a few weak rays of sunlight.

Must be all kinds of holes in that roof, she muttered to herself as she carefully avoided stepping on a good-sized patch of bright green shoots of what she was sure was poison ivy. Years ago, she'd gotten mixed up with that wicked plant and suffered from the encounter for weeks afterwards.

"Can't we stop a minute? I'm clear out of breath again," Dottie pleaded as she lurched around the corner of the house, taking care not to get caught on the sharp nails that stuck out at odd angles from the posts propping up a section of the roof. She was darned if she was going to traipse through all those weeds. Might be full of some kind of bugs for all she knew.

Rab was already out of sight, so there was no choice but to follow. The weeds were thicker here, among them some dried-up thistles loaded with nasty-looking spikes. CeeCee was glad she was still wearing the paint-splattered pants she'd put on that morning to help Dottie do some spring cleaning. Less chance of getting badly scratched. She took a deep breath. The pungent smell of the pines beyond the house reminded her of the home in the country she and Hink had shared, now enjoyed by someone else. She quickly pulled herself together and concentrated on where she was walking.

By the time the women reached the back of the house, the pup was running wildly around in circles, while Jesse was trying to shinny up a large maple tree where the remains of a tree house perched invitingly on a limb.

"Look up there! Something I always hoped Pop would build for me", he said, slipping back to the ground again.

"Careful there, Jess! The whole thing could come down on your head," cautioned CeeCee who was sure she was more aware of what kids could get into than the other two.

Rab was waiting for them near a bench made from a plank laid across two tree stumps.

"I rigged this here seat up special for you, Dot. Sit down an' take a load off. Let's see what I brought us." He unhooked the canvas bag from his shoulders and set it on the ground. Reaching in, he took out a stack of cups and a thermos. A small package of chocolate biscuits followed.

"Time for a break, I'd say," and he separated the cups and unscrewed the thermos lid. Steam rose up as he filled the cups. "Like a coffee there, young Jess?"

Jesse gave up trying to climb the tree. Swiping his hands on his pants, he came over and took a couple of biscuits from the package offered to him by Dottie who was so glad to find a place to sit down, it didn't matter that the bench was a little saggy in the middle. Her weight made it sag a little more.

"Mom doesn't like me drinkin' coffee much, says it makes me too jumpy," Jesse mumbled around a mouthful of biscuit, "but I really like it.

Black like this. Nothing in it." His dusky face shone with sweat. He was feeling much better after the long walk.

"Only way to drink it," agreed CeeCee, who didn't want to take a chance on the bench but was leaning against one of the trees. The strange feeling persisted and seemed to be getting more intense.

Just as Jesse realized the pup was nowhere to be seen, they heard a sharp bark, followed by a string of yelps. Jesse dropped his cup and took off in the direction of the bark. They could hear him calling the pup, here Buzzy, here boy, come here, boy, to be answered by a series of barks that sounded muffled somehow. Then silence. And then a call for help.

6
DAFFY'S DILEMMA

She was a nice girl. At least that's what everyone in town said about Daffy Sturgeon. To an outsider, she might have seemed flighty, with her mop of hair looking like it was a stranger to a comb and her voice sounding as if she'd just finished a long distance run and was trying to catch her breath. She dressed in such a haphazard fashion you could easily imagine she'd dipped into a bag destined for the Second Time Around shop. The truth was straightforward: her mother had always told her vanity was a sin, and her father stormed around the house if anyone dared to talk out loud while he was struggling with his weekly sermon. Which had seemed to the young Daffy to be most of the time.

If she'd thought about it, her parents had had too much control over her life. Even after they were gone, she still heard their voices in her head. But then maybe it was like that for everyone, never getting rid of parental influence. There was no denying, however, she was nice. No gossipy matrons had ever nodded and whispered about her over their tea and cake at the Cosy Corner. No boys had ever collected in a nasty little knot, telling each other nasty little stories with her name featured in them.

All through high school she'd been painfully shy, had worn the same faded raincoat day after day, pulling it more closely around her whenever she was forced to stand and answer questions posed by a succession of teachers who thought they could work their special magic on her and give the poor girl some self-confidence.

And her name. How she hated it. Bad enough her last name was the same as a fish. Ugh! Daffy hated fish, any kind of fish, with their slimy scales and baleful eyes. And their smell! Especially when there was a die-off of alewives in the Lake. For weeks, their rotting bodies would litter the beach, keeping swimmers and boaters well out of range. But her first name was even worse. It didn't matter how often her mother assured her that Daphne was a benign character from Greek mythology, she couldn't convince anyone to call her anything but Daffy, the name she'd called herself when she first learned to talk. *I guess most people think the name fits me,* she remembered thinking after one particularly painful day when the kids at school had teased her. Crazy Fishface, they'd called her. *Why couldn't Mother have chosen a prettier name? Like Gloria. Or Cynthia.*

The Sturgeons had landed in the Bickerton area with the first contingent of United Empire Loyalists, long before there was a Bickerton. Back then, the tiny settlement close to the shores of Lake Monogonquin was known as Conkers Corners. But the Conkers hadn't been too happy with the poor soil on the land they'd been allotted, and moved the whole family farther west. Anyway, the Bickertons were a more powerful force in the early days: they'd produced enough sons to settle one in each of the trades necessary to the continued existence of the fledgling community.

According to the town's official history, which reposed in a couple of apple crates under the back stairs in the Town Hall, Osbert Bickerton was a pretty mean blacksmith, while Edmond ran the Bickerton Inn with its dingy but popular tavern. Samuel kept the general store stocked with a selection of food staples, dry goods and horse remedies. Most of the general store was still standing. Smale's Market had been built onto the front of it. Young Johnny Bickerton operated the saw mill up by the creek, while the head of the clan, John Tremblay, known as J.T., made sturdy boots and shoes. These were the most needed items of all, as the settlers had been given only one pair of boots each, which didn't last long under the punishment meted out by the winter weather. J.T.'s daughters were also plentiful, with no less than six girls arriving at regular intervals, until having had enough of constant childbearing, Sarah Bickerton gave up and died at thirty-nine. And so, as generations of Bickertons continued to prosper, when the time came to satisfy the requirements for establishing a post office, Bickerton was the obvious choice for a permanent name.

The Sturgeons, on the other hand, wielded their power, such as it was, from the pulpit. The earliest Sturgeon was a Circuit Rider, whose once yearly arrival in the widely scattered settlements was welcomed, not only because of the Good News he brought, but because of his legal right to conduct marriages, conferring respectability on couples and their offspring. Old Leviticus Sturgeon would never be rich, or even well-to-do, having to 'subsist on offerings of eggs, the occasional chicken', and 'baskets of fruit and vegetables (in season)', it said in the town history. His sons were too backward, his daughters too plain for J.T. to allow any mingling of their blood with that of the Bickertons.

But generations of Sturgeons persevered in spite of it. That is, until Daffy's time. Too late in life, her mother had died in childbirth in a final attempt to supply the Sturgeons with a male heir. The baby, another girl, was stillborn. Her father, Old Preach, was the last of his line. And there wasn't much hope of any Sturgeon blood being carried on where Daffy was concerned. She was rarely seen at social gatherings, preferring the company of her dogs which went everywhere with her. Her job as church secretary at Saint Peeps, which included keeping the books, was all she wanted. The only time she seemed to lose her shyness and burst forth was when it concerned the church and its shaky finances.

Daffy hadn't been too keen to let the editor of the *Bugler* in on all the gory details of the need for a special meeting, even though she knew perfectly well it would all have to come out. But later, rather than sooner, if she had anything to do with it. She still couldn't believe it herself. The new minister, who had seemed so right for the small but dedicated congregation at Saint Peeps, might just turn out to be what her father would have called a wrong 'un.

Some time ago, Daffy found a strange letter in among the church mail, a letter that looked like one of those poison pens she'd read about in English whodunits. Other letters followed at intervals of a week or so. Not that they were directed at her or anyone in particular. Nor was there any way of telling where they'd come from, as they'd appeared, unstamped and unaddressed, in the box along with the regular mail. Not much to them either. Just a single line on each one, scrawled on plain paper with TO WHOM IT MAY CONCERN across the top. 'HE is not what he seems.' 'HE is a fallen angel.' And then 'Lock up your daughters.' Daffy couldn't help smiling at that one. 'Show him the door before we tell ALL' was the latest. Each one read more and more like lines taken from an old-time melodrama.

The whole thing was incredible to the secretary who was short on imagination when it came to shady doings. After all, this was Bickerton, where hardly anything of any account ever happened. Not to mention the Denton murder of course. Anyway, the Dentons were outsiders so they didn't count. Daffy was too nervous to show the letters to anyone, especially to the Town Constable, Augusta Spilsbury, who had been in her high school class. Daffy had always been intimidated by the tall and clever Gussie Noble. No, the letters would have to remain her secret. At least, for now.

She wondered what it would be like to get letters in the mail. Or at least one letter. Thinking about it, she realized she'd never received a single personal letter in her life. All the mail she ever got was bills and flyers. Everyone she knew was right here. In town. The only relatives she had were some distant cousins in the U.S. Come to think on it, she didn't even know which state. That was all her father's fault. He'd never seen eye to eye with his only brother who left home at nineteen, swearing they'd never see him again. And they hadn't. His sister had left the year before to marry someone the older Sturgeons didn't approve of. She became a member of some weird religious cult her husband belonged to and had kept in touch with Old Preach for a year or two, during which she had two children. Then silence.

But wait a minute, girl. Daffy paused as she fiddled her key into the flimsy lock on the side door of the church hall. *Is the esteemed Reverend Essery really a cousin of old Mrs. Roxton? Or isn't he?* The Roxtons had once owned the biggest house in town, way up on the Hill. Daffy remembered taking notes at the interview session with him when the church elders had waited for three applicants for the position of minister for Saint Peeps and the other two never showed up. And then Jim Arkell, the chairman, saying something about them looking into 'that cousin thing'.

Two days later, a tree he was cutting fell on him and Jim was laid up in Dunhampton Hospital for weeks. By then the church elders had decided to try out the lone applicant and had been so impressed with the Reverend Essery's pulpit-pounding style of preaching, they'd ignored everything else in their eagerness to hire him before another church could spirit him away.

Ministers are sure not easy to come by in a small place like Bickerton, Daffy mused, quickly riffling through the letters she'd retrieved from the church's mailbox, hoping another strange letter would not be among them. *Nope. Only the usual requests for money. Must think we're rolling in the stuff. But still, I wish we could offer more of a salary to our clergymen and not lose them to the wealthier congregations in the bigger towns.*

As she edged through the heavy door to the church office, the telephone on her desk began to ring. Dropping the mail, she snatched the phone off its cradle. Before she had a chance to say "Saints Peter and Paul Union Church, good morning", a coarse voice was saying, "… gotten our letters? We meant what we said" and the line went dead.

7
JESSE GETS A JOLT

"Oh Mom, it was scary, it was really scary, Mom, you oughtta've been there, the pup, I mean Buzzy, um, he fell into this big hole, um, up past this old house, an' well, Mister Rab, he told me it's okay to call him Mister Rab, not Mister Kibbidge, anyways Mister Rab told me to go get a rope, yeah, a rope, outta his truck, under the front seat, an' I did, an' then Mister Rab tied it round me, an' he said I hadda brace him, an' I did, an' well, he hadda go down, in the hole, I mean, an' haul Buzzy up, an' Buzzy was whinin' an', well it was real scary, I mean the whole place was scary!"

"Hey there, Jess, slow down a minute, will you?" Trying to stay calm, Kitty took her son by the shoulder and eased him onto one of the kitchen chairs. *The pup fell into a hole? Up past an old house? A rope? What was the boy on about? Good thing I sent Albie out for groceries. He hates it when Jess gets overexcited.* "What place? Where? You'll have to start again, buddy, you lost me back there."

Kitty lowered herself carefully onto the chair opposite her son. His mud-streaked face made him look darker than he was. Wisps of dried grass poked out from his curly mop. And his clothes were covered with bits of tree bark. Where on earth had the Kibbidges taken the boy? And brought him back in this state. She glanced down at the pup, snuffling under Jesse's chair. The little guy seemed okay even if his normally coal black fur did look a bit dusty. Maybe she should have asked CeeCee where they were going. The Kibbidges were always so offhand about things. *Guess*

I'll find out eventually, and anyway, my boy is home safe and sound, that's the main thing. So what am I worried about?

"Can I have a drink of water, Mom, or even a cola? My stomach doesn't feel so good." Jesse reached down to scratch the backs of his legs. He must have gotten into some brambly thing on the way back to the truck. He *knew* he should have worn his jeans. Too late now. He wasn't all sure he wanted to go back to that place. Even with both Kibbidges and Miz Denton. It was too spooky there. Coming back through the woods in the late afternoon reminded him of that awful day when he'd been trying to get into the Hidden Swamp to look for the Great Blue heron and stumbled over the boot with the orange sock and … Forcing the unwanted image out of his mind, he looked up to see why his mother hadn't answered him. He was startled to see her bent over the sink, clutching the edge of the counter.

"Mom, Mom, what is it, what's wrong?" Jesse scrambled out of his chair. "Mom, hey, maybe you'd better sit down. Your face's real pale and your eyes are all red. Where's Pop at anyways?" He was scared all over again. This wasn't the first time he'd seen his mother do this, but the other times she just said she was okay. He was starting to think there must be something wrong. But why wouldn't his parents tell him instead of trying to hide it? He was almost a teenager now, old enough to be told the truth. Was his mother sick or …?

There was the sound of heavy footsteps on the back porch and the pup let out a low growl. The kitchen door banged open and Albie burst into the house carrying two fat grocery bags.

"Hey there, Soldier, wait 'til you see what I brought us. Kitty, uh, Kitty doll, hold on there!" Albie plumped the bags on the table as he realized something was wrong with his wife. The pup popped out from under the chair and began barking wildly, adding to the confusion. Albie managed to catch Kitty just as her legs went out from under her. Grasping her around the waist, he guided her over to lie her down on the old couch they kept in one corner of the kitchen.

"Jess, run and call the doc, will you, I don't like the look of this. Here, Kit, let's get rid of these, shall we?" Albie bent down and slipped off her shoes. He massaged her feet for few minutes, then grabbed the afghan off the back of the couch and tucked it around her. All Kitty could do was moan.

"Oh, Albie, I feel so stupid. I could feel it coming on and I couldn't do a thing …"

"Shush, shush, quiet now, it's going to be okay, going to be okay now," Albie's deep voice slid down another octave, as he strained to hear Jesse's voice on the phone, saying 'Mrs Woodcock is having another bad spell' as he'd been told to do. They'd practised it a few times so Jesse would know what to do in case Albie wasn't home.

"Maybe we'd better tell the kid, eh? It's not fair to keep it from him any longer, what do you say, eh Kit?" Albie said, looking down on his wife. Since lying down, her colour was improving.

Kitty opened her eyes. She was glad to see Albie. He was so strong and yet gentle at the same time. The frown on his dusky face told her how worried he was. "If you think that's best," she whispered, smiled weakly at her husband and closed her eyes again.

8
IS IT JUST GOSSIP OR …

Two days after the adventure in the woods with the Kibbidges, CeeCee woke up with what she called one of her heads. Meaning a king-size headache. She was puzzled for a moment and then she remembered that much against her better judgement she'd agreed to go out with Mr. Broadkey again. She'd seen him so often during the weeks he'd been trying to sell her house, she'd gotten used to him being around.

But what had she been thinking when she'd agreed to have dinner with him? And for the third time? The good part was that he was the exact opposite of Hink in every way. Every way that counted with her. There was only one hitch. As far as she knew, Hink had never smoked, while Mr. Broadkey was in the habit of hauling out a cigar after dinner. At least he waited until they'd both finished their meal. Although he made a serious effort not to let the smoke drift her way, just the sight of those ugly, smelly things reminded her of how her father used to light one up at the table before she and her mother were finished eating. It always made her feel ill.

What a silly reason not to want to go out with someone just because he smokes cigars. Stogies, we used to call them. Mr. Broadkey is really a very nice man. He had done such a good job of selling CeeCee's house, of getting her a good price for the place in spite of the slow market at the time, that she felt obligated to him. The first few times he'd called to ask her out, she'd refused, saying it was too soon after Hink's death. But Mr. Broadkey had persevered. In a firm, but gentle way, of course. He was too smart to do otherwise.

"Not as if I was a rich widow. Or good looking. Or anything like that. I'm just me. Plain old CeeCee. Grey hair. Wrinkles. Don't know why he bothers," she'd confided to Dottie, one afternoon after having accepted his invitation to dinner yet again.

Dottie snorted. "Looks has got nothin' to do with it, lovey. Nothin' a-tall. Anyways, ya got real kind eyes. An' a nice smile. An' dress nice. An' yer fun to be with. That's what he's after, good company. Yer never dull, always goin' on with somethin'".

Going on with what? Since Hink had been gone, she'd taken only one trip longer than a weekend with one of her girls down to Niagara Falls. And started up the Knittin' Bin. But that was something she and Dottie had done between them. It was true she did enjoy a good joke and a carry-on with the Kibbidges. And she loved trying out new places to eat. And new dishes.

Mr. Broadkey now. He'd asked her to please call him Gene. Short for Eugene, he'd told her. But she couldn't bring herself to get that familiar with him. He'd had a wife who'd run off with another real estate salesman. Happens a lot in our business, he'd said. Divorce. But that was ages ago, he told her, and he wasn't planning on moping around for the rest of his life. Last week when he called, CeeCee had been feeling particularly lonely, missing Hinky, but having to get his photograph out of the dresser drawer now and then to remember just exactly what he looked like. She couldn't believe she was forgetting that.

"It happens, lovey. Oh my yes. It happens," Dottie said, when she'd caught CeeCee with Hink's picture in her hand. "I mind my old auntie who lost her fi-nancy what was in the War, she hadda keep his pitcher right out in front on 'er bureau. She said his face was fadin' away from her." She didn't dare tell CeeCee it was no old auntie, but herself. Donald wasn't quite her fiancé but they'd planned to marry after his flight training was over. But then he was killed in a stupid accident. On the final day. After that happened, she'd given up the idea of marriage to anyone. But she didn't think this was a good time to tell CeeCee her story.

Some comparison, CeeCee thought. *Hink and I were married for over forty years. Not the same as a fiancé, not by any stretch. I couldn't bear having Hinky watching my every move. Even if it was just from a photograph.*

One good thing about Mr. Broadkey, though. He had no interest in birds. No running off to God knows where to add some bird to his Life List. He liked good food, good music, even said he'd like to take her dancing, an activity Hink loathed. Said he wasn't going to look like some jumping jack. Wouldn't even allow dancing at their wedding. Said it had no place in a wedding reception. When she did allow herself to think about it, life with Hink *had* been on the dull side. He'd been so regular in his habits, there was no room for spontaneity. No going out for dinner unexpectedly. No unplanned jaunts. No last minute anything. Except for birding.

Two cups of coffee later, CeeCee felt much better. The thing was, she'd made an appointment with Maybelle to have her hair restyled and she'd promised Dottie to find out about the choir at the old church in Bickerton. Dottie was all keen to find a place to sing with other people. She didn't know why she hadn't thought of a church choir sooner.

Down at the Bo-Tay Salon, in the middle of her comb-out, CeeCee happened to mention the choir at Saint Peeps to Maybelle, who was the town's repository of gossip.

"Oh yeah, they're goin' pretty good now. Or so I hear." Maybelle's freshly hennaed hair was so short, it could have been called a brushcut. The steeply arched brows over her prominent eyes gave her a perpetually startled look. "They tell me not too much singin' was goin' on there after Old Preach passed on. Nobody had the heart. But with this new preacher fella … what for do you want to know?" she asked, swinging the chair around to check that she'd cut the two sides of CeeCee's hair evenly. "Fancy doin' a little warblin', do you?" She swung the chair back.

"Not sure yet. Just want a look-see. Don't want to get involved with the church or anything. Just want to sing." CeeCee peered at her reflection, trying not to squint. She hated the idea of herself in glasses, but knew the day wasn't far off when she'd have to give in. The new hairstyle Maybelle had given her took years off her age. Or so she thought.

"I hear you've been seein' that nice Mister Brody. Good lookin' fella, that one. Is that why you're here? Prettyin' up for a hot date tonight?" Maybelle chortled at her own wit.

CeeCee ignored the jibe. And the mistake in the name. Maybelle was good for finding out things from, but needed no fuel to stoke her already insatiable curiosity. CeeCee slipped off the chair as the hairdresser ran a whisk lightly over her neck and whipped off the protective cape.

"Watch out for that new fella. The preacher I mean. I hear he's got wanderin' fingers," was Maybelle's parting shot as CeeCee escaped to the street.

Wandering fingers? Surely there wasn't a problem with the minister. After all, ministers don't do things like that. Or do they?

9
HUNG OVER!

"Well, are y'all set for tonight, lovey?" Dottie asked, in her cheery first-thing-in-the-morning voice. An early riser, she already had two loads of laundry out on the line and was passing through the kitchen to fetch a third. She'd heard CeeCee come home in the wee small hours, as her old Mam had called it, and had been wondering when her friend would put in an appearance. Heard? That wasn't quite the way it had been. CeeCee always came in quietly. Quieter than a mouse, she was. No, it was the deep purr of Gene Broadkey's departing block-long Lincoln that had awakened her.

CeeCee was sitting at the table, still in her housecoat, nursing a mug of coffee thoughtfully brought to her by Rab before he disappeared through the narrow hall connecting the kitchen to his store out front. It seemed to her Dottie's voice sounded more strident than usual. CeeCee wondered if this was what they meant when people talked about being hung over. It was an entirely new sensation for her. She'd never been able to drink enough to feel the after-effects. Her weak stomach wouldn't let her. But, from the way her head was throbbing and her eyes were refusing to focus, she guessed maybe she was. Hung over. And this headache was ten times worse than the last one.

She tried hard to concentrate on what she'd just heard. Set for what? All she wanted to do right that minute was to crawl back into bed. But that wasn't possible. Not today. A saleslady was coming by soon, expecting their order for the newest patterns and yarns for the Knittin' Bin. And she and Dottie still hadn't worked out just how much of any of it they might need over the summer. A lot depended on what the tourists might be looking for. Cottons, mostly, Dottie thought. Most of the local women knitted only over the long winter months. Too much to do in the summer, what with gardens and picnics and grandchildren to mind. Or rafts of relatives escaping from the suffocating heat of the City and expecting to be entertained all the time.

When CeeCee didn't respond right away, Dottie came over and sat down opposite her.

"My, sure does feel good to get a load off. An' it's, uh," Dottie turned to scan the face of the clock on the wall beside her, "it's only goin' on nine."

CeeCee looked startled. "Are you sure, Dot? Couldn't have slept that late. Could I have?" She struggled to remember what she'd had to drink the night before. Gene had taken her over to Dunhampton, to another new place, said it was run by someone hoping to cash in on the coming tourist invasion. Only been in business a month, you know. They take the money and run, he'd told her with a wry smile. He knew the owner, had sold him the place last year. Donnington House, it was called now, an old house with character.

Another absentee landlord, CeeCee remembered thinking when she was told where they were going. *Never take care of the place, it'll go to pot.* But she went anyway and was pleasantly surprised at how good the food was. And the ambience was first class. Stained glass, wine-red walls, polished floors. Proper white linen tablecloths with full-size napkins. Nothing like the place in the East End of the City she and Hink had gone to one time. Tulmadge's was advertised as being located in an 'old house with character'. High ceilings, faded wallpaper, cramped washrooms. A strong smell of burnt onions. The steak and kidney pie had been delicious, but the china and cutlery were all mismatched, the tabletops full of deep gouges. The whole place had given off a damp and tired feeling that no amount of good food and wine could dispel. If that was character, well ... But what did she have to drink that left her in such a fuddle this morning? She couldn't even remember coming home.

CeeCee ran her fingers through her hair distractedly and tried to concentrate. Ah, it was coming back to her now. Some new kind of wine, at least new to her. What was it ... oh yes, some German stuff with a funny-looking name. The label was kind of funny too. A small boy being spanked on the bare bottom by what looked like a monk. She'd have to ask Gene what the name was again. They'd enjoyed its mellow taste so much, they'd ordered a second bottle and then felt obliged to finish it.

She looked up to see Dottie grinning at her. Her eyes coming into focus, she suppressed her own grin at the sight of Dottie in her washday gear. Her old blue cut-offs and a plaid shirt, more than likely one of Rab's castoffs, its sleeves rolled up to the elbow, an old hanky with the corners tied in knots clinging to the back of her head, her long gray hair done up in a ponytail, made her look like someone's eccentric aunt. She was one of those lucky people who didn't give a hoot how she looked.

"Musta bin some date. You look a sight, girl. Gettin' serious, is it, lovey?" Dottie teased. She was fonder of CeeCee than she'd ever admit, and hated the idea of that slick Mister Broadkey taking her away from them.

"Think I had a touch more wine than I'm used to. Have to be more careful. Wouldn't want Gene to get the wrong idea," CeeCee said, hoisting herself to her feet. She felt the need of something solid in her stomach and groped around in the breadbox, hoping one of Dottie's fruit buns was lurking in the back.

Wrong idea? Humph! What about him, *plyin' her with all that fancy stuff?* Dottie kept that thought to herself and said aloud, "Must be gettin' serious, for certain sure. I found some flowers in the bathroom this morning. Flowers means serious. Ta me anyways."

"Oh, go on, Dot! Not to me they don't." Deftly changing the subject, CeeCee said, "What are we going to tell that lady from the Woollen Works?" She really didn't want to talk about her relationship with Gene. Not now. Not even with Dottie. That was private. And still at a fragile stage. What was that old song ... *'nice and easy does it'*. She enjoyed herself when they were together, and he obviously enjoyed her company, but that was miles from a real courtship. And even farther from marriage. They hadn't known each other that long and anyway, they weren't kids, rushing into something they might be sorry for later on. CeeCee wasn't sure she wanted to get married again. Getting used to one man was one thing. She didn't know if she could go through that again.

"Wait 'til I get the book that woman left us, uh, Joanie, I think was her name." Dottie went into the parlour where she kept the files on the

Knittin' Bin. *Guess I better mind my own beeswax. I don't want to upset CeeCee none. She's a real good friend.*

Coming back with the catalogue, she said again, "It's tonight. The party for the choir. Hadya forgot?"

CeeCee thought for a moment. "Are you sure you want to go?" she said, hoping Dottie would say no.

"Are ya funnin' with me, lovey? Sure, I wants to go. I wouldn't miss it."

CeeCee sighed. "Let's take another gander at that catalogue," she said, sitting back down at the table with a buttered bun in her hand.

10
PARTY TIME!

"Do you think Rab is serious about buying that old farm place we went to, when was it, can't remember just exactly when…" *Am I getting that forgetful, or is there just too much on my mind?* CeeCee gave herself a shake.

"Just into May, I rec'llect, lovey," interrupted Dottie, as she and CeeCee headed out for a party to wind up the choir year. "Yep, he said he'd let us know next week. Somethin' 'bout a well. He's not sure where it's at."

It was nearing the end of June and the weather was glorious: a warm and scented evening, with the daylight still lingering beyond the hills to the west of them. To CeeCee, it didn't seem possible so much time had gone by since she'd moved in with the Kibbidges. At times, her old life with Hink was like a half forgotten dream. Strange how she didn't miss him all that much. She'd been kept so busy, she'd had no time to carry on her research into local history. Organizing the Knittin' Bin had taken more work than she'd figured. And when Dottie suggested they sing in the choir at Sts Peter and Paul Union Church, she didn't see how they were going to find the time. They'd only been with the group for a couple of months and now the choir year was over until fall.

The church everyone called Saint Peeps intimidated CeeCee the first time she saw it. The oldest of the several churches in Bickerton, it was also the most imposing. Up until now, she'd been afraid to go inside the place, but with Dottie along, maybe it wouldn't be so bad. That first night, they hadn't known what to make of it all. They didn't phone ahead, they just showed up on time. But no one asked them to audition. No one asked if they had any previous experience in choir singing. No one even asked if they planned to join the church. They were accepted from the beginning as if they'd always been there. Considering some of the cold-shoulder treatment CeeCee had received as a newcomer, this was a welcome change. But unusual. Talking it over on the way home, Dottie said they must have been hard up to find singers or it wouldn't have been so easy.

The choir leader came in late and had been in for some good-natured ribbing by the male members of the group. One of the ones doing the teasing was an elderly gentleman wearing a baseball cap on top of what looked like a toupée. It had a tendency to slide around when he was talking, making CeeCee feel like laughing, only she didn't dare.

"Couldn't git the milkin' done quick enough, eh? Better get them cows in earlier next week. What's happened to Chuck, taken off on yuh agin, eh? The lazy lug." This banter went on for the first five minutes or so, with a lot of laughing and joking going on between leader and choir. They didn't get down to the business of singing until the gossip had been exhausted and it was discovered the minister hadn't gotten around to giving the leader the list of hymns for the upcoming Sunday.

"Let's just sing some old favourite for our opening hymn, then," said the leader, a short muscular fellow in overalls and a shirt missing its sleeves. His round face was edged with a stubbly beard and topped with a fringe of pale brown hair. His even paler brown eyes had a lively expression in them, as he peered at the group over the top of those quaint half-glasses that had just come into style. His name, as it turned out, was Dix, and he seemed to be continually on the move, full of restless energy. "Anyone got any suggestions?"

"Old Rugged Cross," said Dottie and CeeCee together, then looked at each other sheepishly. "Just popped into my head," whispered Dottie, and CeeCee whispered back, "Same here!"

"Well, well, some new faces, I see," responded Dix, stopping midstride and rising up on his toes, "Stand up there, will you, and introduce yourselves. Sorry I didn't see you before."

"That's 'cause we bin hidin' in the back row," mumbled Dottie and stood up, pulling CeeCee to her feet. "Uh, I'm Dottie Kibbidge an' this here's my friend, CeeCee Denton. We're from over to East Thorne."

"Oh, I know who you are," said a young woman in the front row, turning to stare at them. "Hey, everyone, this lady's brother's the guy with the store over to East Tee. Stayed open real late to help everyone when they had that flood, winter before last. My cousin, Floyd it was, told me all about it. He was one a those got stocked up good that night. Glad to see you."

The others smiled a welcome and started hunting through their music bags, marked with an entwined *PP*. CeeCee held her breath, waiting for someone to say, 'and that's the one whose husband was murdered,' but Dix was already hunched over the keyboard of the ancient upright piano that stood in one corner, striking the opening chords of the song.

Without any preamble, the group launched into a pretty fair rendition of the tune, Dottie and CeeCee following their parts on the worn hymn-books passed across to them by their neighbours. To CeeCee's ears, the harmonizing left much to be desired as two of the four tenors, who were obviously twins, with identical curly grey hair and enormous blue eyes, went their own way and added notes that weren't there.

"But it all worked, didn't it, lovey?" said Dottie later that first night, "and so did everythin' else. I knew ya wasn't that all fired keen on goin', but they were some friendly 'n made us feel real welcome, didn't they, CeeCee? Specially that Dix. Warn't it some big church? Never really looked at it before."

CeeCee had to agree. The building was rather imposing and redolent with history, if you took the time to read all the plaques and dedications hanging on the walls. Faded flags representing various local organizations drooped on either side of the choir loft, while an enormous painting of *The Last Supper* on the wall over the altar was the first thing that caught the eye.

When it came to the Sunday services, CeeCee felt a little strange, it had been so long since she'd had anything to do with a church. Hink had no use for organized religion. Said all they wanted was your money. And now, in her new life, Sunday mornings had usually been taken up with work at the store. The Knittin' Bin had turned out to be such a big hit with local knitters, she and Dottie were too busy during the week to do a good tidy-up and keep the yarns and patterns neatly organized. Never mind helping Rab restock his shelves.

The new minister at Saint Peeps, a Reverend Simon Essery, was a big man who rarely smiled and took his position very seriously. Almost too much so, as far as Dottie was concerned. He had the alarming habit of unexpectedly pounding the pulpit with his fist in the middle of his sermons. Every Sunday, Dottie complained that it got on her nerves. But it didn't disturb CeeCee. Quite the opposite. She was fascinated by the reactions of the people in the congregation. From their perch in the choir loft, she and Dottie had a front-row seat to all the goings-on below them.

A healthy number of the church members were farmers from the surrounding countryside. A ruddy-faced lot, they looked decidedly uncomfortable in stiff white shirts and ties, their good suits straining at the shoulders from the muscles they'd built up from years of heavy farm work. They were accompanied by their wives, who sat primly in their Sunday-best dresses and hats, some even sporting white gloves. Their offspring were nowhere in sight, having been dropped off at the Sunday School in the basement.

Shouting 'Hallelujah' after the scripture readings and 'Amen' after the prayers, the men invariably nodded off during the sermon, only coming to with a start when the Reverend Essery got to the hellfire and damnation part and its pulpit-pounding accompaniment. Week after week, the threat of the afterlife which lay ahead for sinners was his main theme.

A choir member had been assigned to set a large glass of water on the side of the pulpit, from which the reverend took quick gulps in between railing at his flock. One Sunday he got so carried away, he sent the glass flying off the pulpit. It hit the communion table and landed with an audible crack on the wooden floor, the water splashing over the feet of those brave enough to sit in the front row. The reverend went right on ranting as if nothing had happened. CeeCee strained to make out the expression on his wife's face. No such luck. Wilbertina Essery chose to sit in the back of the church under the shelter of the balcony. That morning, her face had been made more difficult to see by her enormous yellow hat with its floppy brim.

"Put out that lotta hellfire, that's for sure," was Dottie's only comment, while CeeCee was nearly sick with the laughter she'd had to suppress until they were safely in the car.

The choir party was being held at Dix's dairy farm, a couple of miles up the road from the church. "Close, but not too close," was his remark when he gave them directions. For her contribution to the potluck supper, Dottie had made her special East Coast lobster stew, leaving a bowlful behind for Rab's supper, while CeeCee had filled two double-crust pies with fresh strawberries, pie crust made by Dottie.

Everyone was already there when they arrived, crammed into the good front room of the small farmhouse. They were drinking fruit punch and passing around little dishes of salted nuts and caramel corn.

"Hey! You made it! Good," said one of the tenors, relieving them of their food offerings and directing them to the punch bowl on a rickety table at one end of the room. CeeCee wasn't sure if she should drink any, not being too sure what was in it, but Dottie took a sip and told her not to worry. No taste of booze in this stuff. CeeCee could never remember which twin was which, they looked so much alike. She felt like asking them to wear nametags. Jimmy and Johnny, they were, only two of the Jones clan, a huge family with a sheep farm north of town. They might come in handy if Rab had any questions about farming. That is, if he really wanted to buy one.

Drinks in hand, the two newest members of Sts. Peter and Paul Union Church Choir joined the others and looked for someplace to sit.

"Here, push over, Ruthie, Jennie, let these two East Tee'ers in," rumbled the thrilling voice of one of the basses. At least it was thrilling to CeeCee, who preferred deep rich tones to the sometimes falsetto of the tenors. Squeezed in between the bass and the other tenor, she forced herself to relax and let the conversation wash over her.

"Where's Mollie at tonight?" asked Ruthie, "stuck with the kids again?"

"Nope," said Jennie, "Poor thing's come down with the janders. Heard her man's laid up again with real bad arthur-itis."

While CeeCee was puzzling over this exchange, hoping Dottie would be able to translate, the front door opened with a crash and the Reverend Essery appeared, carrying a box so large it took both his hands to hold it up. Seen minus his clerical robes over a white-collared vest, in regular clothes he looked just like any of the farmers in the area. Heavy-set and dark-haired, with a bulbous nose flanked by dark deep-set eyes under bushy brows, he could appear quite intimidating. Plunking the box down on the nearest table, he said in his booming voice, "Good evening, all. Hope I'm welcome to join the party. I brought some of my good wife's axle cakes."

There was a momentary drop in the level of the conversation as Dix came in from the kitchen wearing an apron with a pair of colourful birds on the front. "Why not," he said, wiping his hands on his hips, "the more the merrier, I always say."

"Is Daffy here?" asked the reverend looking around the room. "Daffy said she might be here."

"Uh no, uh, well Daffy, she can't stand crowds, she never comes out to do's like this," replied Dix, retrieving the box and disappearing back into the kitchen.

"Hates crowds, always has," remarked the other tenor from the depths of his chair.

"Some crowd. Must be all of fourteen here," rumbled the bass.

"Maybe she can't cook," sniggered one of the sopranos.

Good-hearted Dottie thought that was a mean thing to say, but didn't want to make an issue of it, knowing her friend CeeCee wasn't all that fond of cooking herself. CeeCee wasn't paying too much attention. She was still trying to figure out what kind of illness the janders was. *And arthur-itis? And axle cakes? Looks like I've a whole new language to learn. Wonder if there's a dictionary of country lingo. Thought I knew a lot of it but ...*

She turned to ask Dottie if she knew what it all meant when Dix poked his head out from the kitchen and announced in a loud voice, "Come and get it, folks. You all know I'm world famous for my potlucks." He snorted at his own wit.

"Aw, pull the other one, Dix, I kicked the slats out of my cradle laughin' at that one."

CeeCee couldn't see who the speaker was, as they shuffled out to the kitchen where a mountain of food was waiting to be demolished. Everything was delicious to CeeCee, especially the corn pudding. She was relieved to see that axle cakes were the good old Eccles cakes her grandmother used to bake and not some oily and indigestible concoction. When she returned to the kitchen for some coffee, she saw the plates her pies had been in were both empty. And so was Dottie's lobster pot.

After supper, they enjoyed a singsong, which Dottie joined in with gusto. CeeCee thought she'd be content to observe her fellow choir members, but jumped in quick enough when someone started the old round 'Fire's burning'. However, she did think it odd that whenever the reverend appeared, the joking and joshing stopped abruptly. Luckily for the party, he'd left soon after the food was gone. *Wonder what's up with him? He's a real wet blanket. Doesn't seem to want anyone to have a good time. Doesn't have to say a thing. When he shows up, the mood in the room drops like a stone.* She couldn't help remembering a young minister she'd known years ago who played the piano like a dream and enjoyed nothing better than a good joke.

Dottie put her in the picture later on that night when they were washing up the dishes they'd brought home, along with the few Rab had left stacked in the sink.

"Got it from that Ruthie girl. Watch out for our dear reverend in the dark corners, she says. He has trouble keepin' his hands to hisself, she says. Can't be trusted, she says. Says the church board didn't know much about him when they took him on, but now they're wishin' they had," she added mysteriously.

CeeCee said nothing, but when she was ready for bed, she thought maybe she should say a prayer for the Reverend Essery, whatever he'd been up to. After all, wasn't that how a good churchgoer should behave? And why hadn't his wife been with him? As she switched off her bedlamp and tucked her quilt up around her neck, her mind went back to the start of the evening. If Rab was serious about buying that run-down farm property, she wasn't at all sure she'd be able to show any enthusiasm for the project. There had been a decidedly strange feeling in the air that day, a feeling of dread. Something bad must have happened there.

11
LADY IN BLUE

Ever since the possibility of buying the abandoned farm had occurred to him, Rab seemed quieter somehow. Both women noticed it. He never was much of a talker at the best of times, but when he was involved in a new project, he would be asking his sister's opinion all along the way. "Hey, Dot, so waddya think, Dot? Sound okay to you?" Back when he'd been planning to leave home, he was after her almost daily, needing her okay to leave her alone with their old Mam. But she knew he had to find work. Somewhere else.

This time was different. This time she had no idea what he was thinking, never mind planning. Nary a peep out of him other than good morning or good night. Had he found out something he didn't want her to know? Was he having second thoughts about the old place? And just what *had* happened there years ago anyway? Or was it one of those tall tales that grows taller with each telling? When Buzzy fell into the well that day, she'd been so relieved they'd gotten him out, she'd never stopped to think why he hadn't fallen all the way down. Or was it, in fact, a well? In the midst of the confusion, with Jesse hollering and the dog yelping, she'd tried to ask Rab what had happened exactly. But he'd just told her and CeeCee to stay away, it wasn't safe. No more than that.

She thought some more about that first day. She didn't want to say anything to spoil her brother's enthusiasm, but the place had given her the creeps. She'd been relieved to discover that CeeCee felt the same way. Since Rab had done all the wheeling and dealing with the town officials

– the property had some problems connected with it, something to do with back taxes or liens or whatever – she felt left out. Stuff like that just made her head spin. She'd never been good at arithmetic and was glad CeeCee was. On account of the Knittin' Bin.

Another odd thing she'd only just noticed. Whenever she was over in Bickerton, people on the street, people she'd never met, stared at her when she passed them. She wondered if that was how it was with young Jesse, him being different from the rest of the folks. To be singled out as someone who didn't quite fit in. She could see it with Jesse having a white mother and a black father. The only thing different about *her* she could think of was that she never took time to change when she had to go over there. Today she was wearing a green plaid skirt and an old orange sweatshirt with a pink and purple bandana on her head and an ancient pair of Rab's socks. But why hadn't it happened to her sooner? Maybe it had, and she simply hadn't noticed. Or was she just imagining it? That and the uncertainty over the farm were getting to be too much of a muchness, as her old Mam used to say.

How Rab heard about the old farm was a story in itself. One morning at the end of the winter, a customer had come into the store asking for apple cider. Rab didn't make it himself, but his friend Sam down past the Canal did. Sam hinted there might be a secret ingredient in his cider that made it so popular. After one taste, Rab suspected it was simply pear juice. And delicious. As Sam lived too far from the main road, Rab offered to sell the cider for him. He still had a couple of bottles left.

The customer was someone he didn't remember seeing before. When he asked her if she was new to the area, she laughed and said, "New old, you could say. I was born and bred in the old Oates place. You know? Just outside East Tee?" Rab replied *he* must be the newcomer. He'd never heard of any Oates. She laughed again and said, "We've been long gone away from here. I've been in the City all this time. The rest of us are all over tarnation." Rab said it sounded like *his* family, the Kibbidges, and proceeded to tell her how he came to be in East Tee. The lady listened intently and then said her name was Emmalina Oates, but he could call her Mrs. Emma. Everyone did.

As he told CeeCee that night, when Dottie was out in the kitchen busy making soup for the next day, the woman looked like someone out of a fairy tale. "I dunno, but she was sure some different. She had on a skyblue dress what went all the way down to the floor. Long an' silky like. Had some lacy stuff round her neck. White gloves up to her elbows. Big hat with a mass a ribbons, sittin' up on top a white hair. White as snow, it was. Done up like the old Queen Mary's, it was. With these bright blue eyes, well, after she left, I was wonderin' if I'd imagined her."

CeeCee wasn't surprised at the description. "Rab, every town has its characters. One old guy over in Bickerton thinks he's a cowboy. Always wears a Stetson and those funny pointed cowboy boots. Must be hard to walk in. And there's another one who…" Rab shrugged and went off to do something in the store, while CeeCee turned her attention back to the knitting book she'd been reading. But for some reason, Rab had left out a description of the mystery lady's shoes and handbag, like some kind of dull, pebbly leather. Much later, she found out they were over thirty years old and made of ostrich skin.

Rab hadn't told a soul the rest of what happened that day. Business had been slow and he and the old-fashioned lady got to chatting about what was happening to the farms in the area. So many gone. Rab remarked he'd been thinking he should buy one before all the good farmland was swallowed up by the developers who would bury it under houses and such. Like what was happening around Dunhampton. And other towns.

Mrs. Emma was quick to remind him that the people who bought all those houses would have to eat, so he was for sure in the right business. He said well yes, but with the farmers gone, the food would have to come from a long way off and cost more. He still thought he'd like to grow his own vegetables and things, but figured any farmland would be too rich for him when Mrs. Emma surprised him by saying airily, "Well sir, I know of a place most folks don't. No soul has lived there for years. It might just go for taxes owing. That is, if it's still on the books." Then she said in a whisper, "That is, if you had the nerve." Rab was just about to ask her what she meant by nerve when another customer came in. Mrs. Emma plopped down the money for the cider, saying nice-meeting-you-be-back-again-soon and was out the door.

After he'd seen to the new customer, he mentally kicked himself. He'd let the odd little lady get away without telling him just where exactly the farmland was, this place that could be had for cheap. *Must be a catch some-wheres. Nothin' comes cheap without a catch.*

A week or so later, she came back for some tinned soup, bread, butter, eggs and bacon. He'd been able to ask her what he wanted to know before another customer sent her scurrying away. She took a few minutes to reply as if she'd had second thoughts about telling him. She put her purchases down on the counter and said softly, "Well, if you must know, but don't tell another soul, it's way up along past the Lonesome River. But you don't want to go up there. No siree now, that wouldn't be a good idea." She refused to say any more and was gone, leaving Rab to puzzle over why she'd told him about the farm in the first place. He'd just have to wait until her next visit before he could pin her down as to its exact location. After that, he found himself keeping an eye on the door. In case she came back.

12
WITCHING NEEDED HERE

Near the middle of July, the place was his - lock, stock and barrel. Rab was beginning to wonder if he'd made a mistake, taking on the old abandoned farm. Making another trip up there on his own, he hadn't been able to locate a usable well, even though he reckoned a place that size must have had more than one. The well Buzzy had fallen into appeared to be full of rocks. He hoped it wasn't blocked up solid. That would make it next to useless to try and open up. When he tried to find out about the place from the old-timers who hung around the store looking for someone to play cards with, none of them seemed to know anything about it. Or they weren't telling.

As soon as he'd taken title to the old farm, he moved quickly to get the main road in unblocked. No sense trying to put a road through where he'd brought Dottie, CeeCee and Jesse that first time. Too many trees. And that stream to cross. More than likely it would flood in the early spring. Opening the road had taken up what was left of June and run into July before the paperwork could be finished and he could take possession of the place. Someone, whoever that was, wanted to make sure no one could ever get in by road to reach the farm. Even the sideroad leading to the farm lane had been impassable and had to be cleared of the masses of dead trees lying every which way with their rotting trunks surrounded by brush. For Rab, the big question was why. What could have happened there?

The lack of water wasn't his only problem. No power lines. He knew from Jim Arkell the power had come through the area over twenty-five years ago. Some people had held out against it, figuring it was just another government scheme to get their money. After all, oil lamps and wood stoves had been good enough for their ancestors, hadn't they? One good thing: Jim had found both the men and the machinery to clear the sideroad. He was still in poor shape after his tree-cutting mishap, but he seemed to know more about things than the rest of the inhabitants Rab had met. Maybe it was time he went up and visited Jim. He'd take young Jesse with him. It would be good for the boy to learn a bit more about the area. And he had an idea of just how Jesse might fit in with his plans.

It was close to the end of the school year when Rab and Jesse drove up to the Arkell farm. They didn't talk much on the way. Neither of them liked chitchat, but rather enjoyed a companionable silence. So many mailboxes along the Ninth Concession road had the name ARKELL on them, it was a good thing Jim had told him to watch for white flagpole flying a red, white and blue flag. Funny. It looked like a Union Jack. That flag hadn't been in use since the '60s. A large truck was blocking the laneway, so they went to the front door. A solemn-faced brown-eyed woman in a plain gray dress and yellow apron, her ginger hair tied back with a piece of string, ushered them through the kitchen to the back porch that overlooked a big red barn and some smaller outbuildings.

It was a warm summer morning, sunny, breezy, with lots of little white clouds chasing each other across a sky, the blue of which reminded Rab of Mrs. Emma's dress. A bit of the breeze was blowing in the direction of the house, making it obvious that farm animals weren't too far away. Jim was sitting in a wheelchair, trying unsuccessfully to read the local paper the breeze threatened to whip out of his hands. When he saw the visitors, he folded the paper and smiled at them.

"Don't mind me none. I'm stuck here for another coupla weeks, eh Dolly? Let's hope that's all. Dolly's gettin' fed up with my grousin' and grumblin', eh Doll? Dolly here's my sister." The woman smiled faintly and disappeared back into the kitchen. Jim was one of those people who smile a lot. His face was grooved with laugh lines and his light brown eyes sparkled in the sunlight. A few wisps of sandy hair stuck out from under his cap. An old farm dog, lying in the sun at the bottom of the steps, feebly thumped his tail, but made no move to get up. Jim saw Jesse looking at the dog and explained, "This old fella's on his last legs. We're lettin' him take it easy. He was a real good farm dog in his day, he was."

After Jesse told Jim all about his pup, which Rab had suggested he leave behind this trip, and Jim told Jesse all about a pup he'd had when he was Jesse's age, the two men got down to business. Jesse wandered down to the barn to have a look at the new batch of kittens Jim said were in the loft. The old dog thumped his tail again but stayed put. Rab settled himself in one of the old car seats that served as chairs.

"Before I get to what I come for, tell me somethin'. Why're you flyin' the old Union Jack? Hain't seen one a them in donkey's years."

Jim laughed. "That's not a Union Jack, that's a Loyalist flag. It's missin' a set of crossbars. You mind the Loyalists? A ways back, our folks were all Loyalists. They came up an' settled here after they were hounded outta their homes. They had to leave their properties south of the border and escape with what they could carry. Ichabod and Isaac Arkell got this far and decided to stay."

Rab thought for a minute. "Why, no, Jim, don't know as I ever heard that story. I'm from Back East, you know. One day you'll hafta tell me more. But right now …"

"I'd be glad to. But I don't think now's the time either," Jim laughed again.

"Well now, you bin such a help to me so far, can you tell me anythin' about wells? How to find 'em? And how to find water? I heard you got a brother what witches 'em. Could he help me out?"

Jim angled his chair so he was facing Rab. The sun was getting stronger, making it hard for him to see properly.

"Don't tell me you went an' bought the place an' you got no water on her!"

"Looks like it. 'Twas too good a deal to pass up. I knew there'd be a catch somewheres. Always a catch," Rab scratched his head under his cap.

"Well," said Jim slowly, "if she's a done deal, she's done. Yep. I got a brother up to Hickses Corners, way up past Dunhampton, doncha know? He useta witch real good. Could find water in a rock, I allus said. Got the right name for it, too. Aaron. You rec'llect Aaron? In the Good Book? When the good Lord told him to take his staff an' strike a rock in that there desert? And sure enough, there was a heap a water under it?"

"Not much for Bible readin'. Never got the hang of it, somehow." Rab shifted in his seat. Jim noticed his discomfort and went on.

"Is it for sure there's no water in that well you say young Jesse's pup fell in? Gosh, gee whiz, I wish I wasn't stuck here at home. Like to take a look around myself."

"If there is, water, I mean, 'twill take a heap a work to clear out what's blockin' it. Funny thing," Rab said, glad to be off the topic of Bibles, "I got the place for just the taxes an' a bit more. Easy as pie. The guy in the township office looked at me kinda sideways, but never said boo." He cleared his throat. "I ain't ready to quit. Not just yet anyhow. Us Kibbidges er tough."

"Tell you what," said Jim, whose curiosity was growing by the minute. He vaguely remembered hearing stories about the old farm when he was much younger, but never put too much stock in gossip. "Let's you an' me …"

He was interrupted by the simultaneous arrival of Jesse, out of breath after running back from the barn, and his sister, Dolly, with a pitcher of lemonade and some large glasses.

13
SYD STEPS IN

Feeling thoroughly disheartened, Daffy Sturgeon sat at her desk in the dimly lit church office at Saint Peeps. So few people turned out for her emergency meeting, it had hardly been worthwhile setting up the chairs in the Hall. And the letters were still coming. She'd been so sure her notice in the *Bugler* would attract a crowd that she'd been shocked at the poor attendance. Had interest in church affairs fallen so low? Weren't they even just a little bit curious as to what constituted an emergency? One male member of the congregation had been short with her on the phone, saying she was way out of line calling such a meeting. That was up to the Board and not the secretary. Maybe others felt the same way. But the Board seemed oblivious to what was happening. And did they even know? And where was the minister? Gone fishing or some such. Somebody had to do *something*.

She tried to remember what had been going on in Bickerton that night that might have kept them away. Oh dear, maybe it was that new television serial called *Boots* or something. TV hadn't been in the town long enough for the novelty to have worn off. Several times, Daffy caught herself stopping at the sight of the window of Jakes' Furniture and Appliances lit up with half a dozen sets, all tuned to the same show. As she stood there, fascinated by the tiny figures flitting about on the screens without a sound, she could hear Old Preach's voice in her ear, "that there's the work of the devil, that is."

Only five people had taken the trouble to show up that night. Old Mrs. Grimble never missed a meeting if it had to do with her beloved church. The Jones twins from the choir were already seated when she arrived and a few minutes later, Syd Spilsbury slipped in the side door, followed by Sherry Roxton. They waited, chatting quietly among themselves until twenty minutes had gone by. When it was apparent no one else was going to show up, Daffy suddenly remembered they needed a quorum of fifteen to make any decisions,. She'd had to let them go with many apologies. When she went to the side door to turn off the yard lights, she was surprised to see that Syd was still there.

"Okay, Daffy. Don't send me away feeling I've wasted my evening. What's this emergency stuff all about?" He came back into the Hall, giving her an encouraging smile. When she didn't respond, he tried again.

"Come on, Daff. Is it something to do with the new Rev.? I've heard a few rumours, but I didn't pay much attention to them. What is he, an axe murderer or something? Hey, I was only kidding!" he was quick to add, seeing the look on her face.

Not knowing what to do now, Daffy turned and began to move towards her office. She didn't feel she should tell the town's only newspaper what she really suspected. If it got into the *Bugler* before the church members had a chance to hear about it, she'd likely lose her job. And goodness knows what else could happen.

But Syd wasn't giving up that easily. He followed her down the corridor. When she got to her office, Daffy stopped and turned to face him.

"I don't think you should stay. Not when we're alone like this. You know how people talk in this town. You better leave. Maybe I made a mistake calling that meeting. Maybe it's just my imagination, but …" She sighed. How much longer was she going to have to keep her suspicions to herself?

"Come on, Daff, you can tell me. Maybe I can help in some way." Syd could see that she was upset. They stood standing awkwardly on either side of the door. When Daffy went to open it, Syd blocked her way.

"You might have known I'd show up tonight. After all, you asked me to. What's so mysterious that you can't tell me?" He was determined to worm it out of the girl, but he hadn't forgotten how shy she'd been all through high school and how much teasing she'd suffered. It must have taken a lot for her to try to run a meeting. He took a wild guess and said, "I thought everything was okay with this new guy. His wife seems pleasant enough. I don't like to think there's some kind of trouble at good old Saint Peeps." He made a show of shoving his notebook in his back pocket and stowed his pen in its customary place, his shirt pocket. How many times had Gussie scolded him for using cheap pens that left ink spots behind? He wondered if she missed washing and ironing his shirts. Probably not.

"Well," Daffy said slowly. She took a deep breath. "Well, um, it's like this." She looked quickly around. "You better come in. But just for a minute, mind. You see, it's these letters and …". They moved into her office and Daffy carefully closed the door.

When Syd had had a look at the letters, he was shocked. Poison pen letters were only in murder mysteries. Weren't they? Not in a town like Bickerton. Surely not. A headline popped up in front of his eyes: **POISON PEN PESTERS SAINT PEEPS.** *Don't be ridiculous, Syd, you could never ever write that.* The headline faded.

"This looks like a job for the police," he said. "We should take them to Gussie. First thing tomorrow."

But Daffy wasn't about to let the letters leave her hands. She didn't want to show them to Constable Gussie. Or anyone else in authority. Not just yet anyway. She'd hoped when some of the church members heard about it, they'd know what to do. She didn't want to start a scandal if there was some other way of dealing with the situation.

Syd sat down on a bench along the wall, figuring this was going to take some time. To distract her, he started telling Daffy how he felt about religion. He said that seeing the row of classroom doors had brought back memories. The hours he'd spent in those rooms, trying to puzzle out what the Sunday school teachers were telling him. Or what her father, Old Preach, had been on about, near the end of each service, when he shouted from his lofty perch, scaring the young Syd half to death. Or what his parents were always telling him. All of them talked and talked. On and on. About good and evil, about heaven and hell. Read him Bible stories. Showed him pictures of strange men wearing long white robes and sandals, their dark faces obscured by straggly beards.

"When I was a kid, I couldn't see how it mattered what those people, dead and gone for a zillion years, had said or done. I wanted to be outside with my buddies, going down to the Lake to throw stones, or biking out into the countryside, looking for hills to conquer. Not having to put on a shirt and tie and a pair of scratchy dress pants." He smiled at the recollection, then turned serious again. "I got out of going to Sunday school when Mother died and Dad didn't care what I did with myself." He shifted in his seat.

When Daffy went to interject, he hurried on. "Sure. Gussie and I got married. Right here. At Saint Peeps. By Old Preach himself. He'd given us lectures on marriage and what was meant by commitment. But nothing he said helped us to stay together. Nothing that would take all the worry and stress away. Or would stop me feeling guilty I couldn't live up to my Dad's wishes for me and the *Bugler*." Once he'd started, Syd couldn't seem to stop himself from spilling it all out to Daffy, who stared at him without making a sound. "Both of us spent too much time on our jobs. And not enough on each other." There. He'd admitted it. At last.

Sitting alone in her office after Syd left, with the promise to call her the next day, Daffy hadn't known what to think. She'd always thought Gussie and Syd were the perfect couple and had been as mystified as anyone else in town when they'd broken up. Maybe things weren't always what they seemed to be. She had to smile at the thought of her father. Maybe he *did* scare some kids. Maybe that's why they never came to church once they'd grown up. And maybe Syd was right. She should show the letters to Constable Gussie. She'd forgotten to tell Syd about the phone calls. She'd had another one. That morning. Even more threatening than the ones before. Same husky voice. Same heavy breathing.

Remembering it, Daffy felt a sudden chill go down her spine.

14
REVELATION AND RELIEF

Telling Constable Gussie hadn't been such an ordeal after all. Syd had already paved the way for her visit to the police station. Daffy was relieved to find Gussie listened closely to her and didn't ask her questions she couldn't answer. After looking at the letters, Gussie said she wasn't so sure these would qualify as poison pen letters. Those were usually directed at an individual. She didn't think these were something Daffy should have to deal with. Alone. She was more concerned with the anonymous phone calls.

"Are you absolutely sure you didn't recognize the voice?" she asked, treading carefully. She remembered how shy the younger Daffy had been at school and didn't want to frighten her. "Was it a man or a woman's voice, do you think?"

Daffy shuddered. "All I can tell you is the voice sounded the same. Every time. I keep thinking the person," she shivered again, "the person, whoever it is, has got a bad cold. Or some serious throat problem. They never say too much. It's as if their voice won't let them talk very long." She sighed and pulled her jacket more tightly around her, the way she used to do with her trenchcoat at school.

Gussie didn't think that was what was happening here. More than likely, the person was using some device to disguise the voice. To set her at ease, she asked Daffy to leave the letters with her and if any more showed up to let her know right away. As for the phone calls, the next time could she listen really hard and see if there was any kind of noise in the background that might give some idea of where the person was calling from? Daffy said she'd do her best, even though she found those calls upsetting.

Gussie thought that was the end of the conversation, but Daffy surprised her.

"Can I tell you something else? And please, *please* don't let on to …" she glanced around fearfully to see if anyone was within earshot.

Gussie said in her most serious voice, "Nothing will leave these four walls if you don't want it to, I mean, if you don't want it to."

"Well," said Daffy slowly, "I can't help thinking. There's something odd about the new pastor." There. She'd gotten it out, what had been bothering her for weeks. She went on quickly. "You see, he's one of those people who, um, get too close to you. When he's talking to you. He's even backed me up against the wall. More than once." She took a deep breath and went on. "When he does that, his voice gets louder. And, well, his mouth goes all white. With spit, I mean. And his nose, well, his nostrils get bigger and, uh," she stopped again. "Well, he reminds me of nothing so much as a frightened horse." They looked at each other and started to laugh.

"That's the best description I've heard in a long time," Gussie said when she could stop laughing. "Are you sure he isn't just nervous, I mean, just nervous? Or something like that?"

Daffy wiped her eyes. "I wondered about that. At first. But he's been here a while now so that can't be it. Anyway, why would he be nervous with me? Come to think on it. The letters started coming not long after he came. And then his wife showed up a couple of weeks later. Funny thing. I heard she was here for two Sundays before anyone laid eyes on her." She paused. "Peculiar sort of person, *she* is. I don't know what to make of her. She reminds me of a little bird, with her glittery little eyes and her chirpy voice."

A horse and a bird! Funny combination was Gussie's reaction. But she kept the thought to herself. *Had no idea Daffy could be so descriptive.*

When she was alone again, Daffy felt better than she had in weeks. *Gussie will help. I know she will. And didn't she look sharp in that uniform? So professional.* For her part, Gussie had been astonished at the change in the normally timid girl. *Poor thing. Wonder what's going on at Saint Peeps, of all places? Better run a check on these letters. And, well, those phone calls. Don't know for sure what to do about them. This doesn't look at all good.* She was so glad Syd had encouraged the church secretary to come forward before anything really serious happened.

On her way back to the church, Daffy remembered what old Mrs. Grimble had said after the new pastor's wife had finally shown herself. "Odd little thing, isn't she. Do you think she'll be any good to us, Daffy?" But Daffy just mumbled something about waiting and seeing and had gone on her way. She knew she had to be really careful what she said, or even hinted at, about the new occupants of the parsonage. Jobs were hard to come by in Bickerton and she was darned if she was going to let a slip of the tongue ruin hers.

By good, she assumed the woman meant she'd be a help to her husband. A pillar of the Union Ladies' Group. On hand for everything. A dogsbody, always there to pick up the slack. Unfailingly friendly. Smiling. Even-tempered. Uncomplaining. Nice sensible clothes. All the characteristics that were expected of pastors' wives. Daffy was reminded of pastors' wives she'd met at different church functions with her parents. The Rev. Peabody's Midge, who'd worn spike-heeled sandals showing her scarlet toenails. The Rev. Plimpton's Julie, who'd giggled at everything and was so fat she broke two of the springs in the sofa in the church lounge. The Rev. Hubert's Janie, no, Jeanie, who'd gone through at least half a pack of cigarettes before they left. None of these wives would have measured up to what Mrs. Grimble meant when she said 'good'.

Daffy knew only too well what her own mother had had to put up with when her father was still alive. People knocking on the parsonage doors at all hours, demanding to see the reverend. Vagrants looking for a free meal, and turning nasty when they were handed a voucher to get something at the Cosy Corner. Phone calls. Requests for money. Some demands impossible to meet. Never mind the weddings, baptisms, funerals and counselling for which the reverend didn't receive a penny. No holidays for them. There was too much going on for the Sturgeon family to even think about going anywhere.

Still, she couldn't help but feel sympathy for the odd little woman, Mrs. Essery. Her name was Wilbertina. 'Oh please, *do* call me Bertie,' she'd confided, when they were introduced. *Well, whatever sort of woman she turns out to be, people haven't forgotten Mom. For sure, they'll be measuring*

Bertie's performance against hers. Should I warn her about what to expect? Or let her discover the Bickertonian style for herself?

15
JESSE IS WORRIED

Jesse lay sleepless on the narrow cot Mister Rab had set up for him in the little storage room behind the store. He knew he should be dead tired after helping his boss stack firewood all afternoon. His arms felt like they belonged to someone else. Mister Rab said the heavy work would help build up his muscles. He wasn't sure he wanted them built up if it was going to hurt this much.

Buzzy sprawled on his mat beside the cot, his legs twitching every once in a while. Probably dreaming of chasing those pesky rabbits that sometimes came around the store. Jesse would have to keep a close eye on him. Mister Rab said he would knock together a pen for the pup to stay in outside during the day. He'd promised to put it in a shady spot under one of the trees. But with all the extra customers coming from all over, he hadn't had the time yet.

The pungent odour coming from the onions hanging in bunches from a hook in the ceiling filled the room. Jesse loved the smell of onions. It always reminded him of coming home and finding Pop crying over the sink after peeling onions for his chili. He wondered where Pop was now. Not too far away this time, he hoped. And not for too long either.

Jesse was really worried about his mom. He knew *that* what was keeping him awake. This evening when he'd made his usual phone call home, he was shocked when his mother's voice sounded funny. The conversation ended abruptly when Kitty hung up on him. She'd never done that before and Jesse had hurried to find Dottie, who was still in the kitchen putting some beans to soak. All she could give him in the way of comfort was that ladies who were waiting for babies to come sometimes didn't feel like talking. At least she said her old mam had been like that. Lots of times.

Trying in vain to get comfortable on the lumpy mattress, Jesse thought back to the day when he'd come home near the end of school to see a familiar truck parked outside his house. What was Mister Rab doing here? As he came into the kitchen, he heard Mister Rab say, "… if it's all right with you, Missus, that is." The little man with the crinkly eyes was sitting at the kitchen table with a mug of coffee in front of him and talking to Jesse's mom who was fanning herself with an old magazine. They turned to greet him as he slid into his customary chair.

"Here he is," his mother said, smiling at him. "You can ask him yourself. As far as I can see, it would be okay with us."

Dying of curiosity which he tried hard not to show, Jesse waited politely to hear what Mister Rab wanted to know.

"Got a job for ya, young fella," said Rab, his eyes twinkling.

After he heard what Mister Rab had in mind, Jesse didn't know what to say. He sat there awkwardly with Buzzy on his lap, even though his mom had said over and over such treatment would spoil the pup. He knew they were waiting for an answer.

"Well, um, Mo-om" Jesse's voice squawked, something it had been doing a lot of lately. He tried again. "Mo-om, can I, er, um, *may* I take Buzzy with me?" On hearing his name, the pup shoved his head under Jesse's arm, furiously wagging his tail. "I don't think, um, that is, um, I don't want to go without him unless, that is, um, unless you'll be too lonely …"

"Oh no, Jess, you take him, if it's okay with Mr. Kibbidge," Kitty said quickly.

"Please. Just call me Rab, I don't hold with too much fancy stuff." Rab turned slightly towards boy and pup. "Fine with me, long as he don't bark at the customers," he said with a grin. "That's what I like about this young fella, always thinkin' of his mother."

Remembering that day, Jesse struggled to keep the tears from coming. His mom really shouldn't be alone right now. Pop had told them he wouldn't be gone so long this time, maybe just a couple of weeks, so that meant he should be back home the week after next. Jesse sure hoped so.

He hadn't told the Kibbidges yet but Doc Blair said it might even be twins this time. The doctor went on to reassure them and said it was bit early to tell, but still … Jesse shuddered. He was having trouble at the thought of one baby brother. Now there could be two babies! And they might even be girls!

16
DOTTIE GETS AN EARFUL

Dottie had just finished unpacking the latest order of yarn and needles for the Knittin' Bin that had arrived earlier that afternoon, when a woman who looked familiar appeared in the doorway.

"Am I disturbin' anythin'?" asked the visitor. "Remember me? From the choir?"

Dottie wiped her hands on her hips. She'd been hoping CeeCee would show up pretty soon to help her get all the new wool shelved before supper. CeeCee had been spirited away right after lunch by her `gentleman friend`, as Rab called Gene Broadkey, to look at a house he was thinking of buying. *Thinkin` of buyin', my Great Aunt Fanny. Wantin` CeeCee`s sayso before poppin` the question. Which he's bound to do any day soon, the way things have been goin` on between them lately. Hopin` she'll fall for the place an' then he'll buy it for them to live in. It better not be too far away, I sure need her help runnin` this place.* She came to herself with a start. She hadn`t meant to be rude, but what was that woman's name – Jennie? Maisie? No, Ruthie – that was it.

"No, no", she said hastily, "Ruthie, isn`t it. Good ta see ya. I just finished, leastways for now." She pulled two chairs out from behind the counter. "Here, sit down, why doncha, till I catches me breath. I don`t bend over so good any more, an' these here big cartons be too heavy to haul up on the table." Dottie took off her apron and slung it on the back of her chair.

After giving the Knittin' Bin part of the store the once over, the woman moved over to sit down.

"Nice little place you got here," remarked her visitor, who was indeed Ruthie, Ruthie Simmons from over past Bickerton. "I never been in here before, but I heard good things from them that has. My, ain't that hummaditty somethin'?" She took a hanky out of her purse and wiped her face which was well supplied with freckles. Her thick sandy hair was worn in a braid coiled tightly around her head. She was wearing the uniform most of the farm women seemed to prefer – a much laundered flowery cotton dress with a belt to match and short sleeves, knee socks rolled down to her ankles and an old pair of sensible shoes.

"Oh, most of it's my brother's doin'. It's him as has the place. He works mighty hard ta get in what folks wants." Dottie loved bragging about her brother, him being the baby of the family and all.

"Well, I hadda come over to my Auntie Lou's here in East Tee an' happened to remember this is where you was at", Ruthie explained. "I been wonderin', at least, we been wonderin' if you was plannin' on comin' back to the choir when we start again end of August. I know it's only early summer now, but we wanted you to know you're both real welcome. Dix'll give you a buzz when the date is for first practice. Depends on what's happenin' with his farmin'." She mopped at her face again.

"Dearie me, where'er my manners! Would ya like a glass a somethin' cold?" Dottie got to her feet. "I got some real nice lime juice, fresh squeezed an' all, sittin' in the fridge." On her way to the kitchen for the drinks, she wasn't sure she wanted to think that far ahead, but she'd enjoyed singing in a group again. It had been so long since she'd been able to. Since she left home, in fact. Home, where everyone sang. And sang a lot together.

After she'd handed Ruthie her glass and they'd both had a good swig of the refreshing juice, Ruthie leaned a little closer.

"I hope you don't mind if I tell you somethin'," she leaned even closer, "but we thought you two should know. Someone's back in town we never thought to see again. This person useta sing with us in the choir, oh, years and years ago. And now she's back, she's bound to show up to sing again."

Dottie wondered what in the world the woman was on about. What was wrong with wanting to come back to the choir? She scrootched around on her chair and waited.

"You see, it's like this. Oh she has a good voice an' all, but … " Ruthie's voice trailed off. She picked at an invisible thread on her dress.

"Yes?" Dottie said, scarcely daring to take a breath. "And?"

"Well," said Ruthie, hunching closer, "you see, when you get right down to it, well, she's a bit odd, like." She pursed her lips together and sniffed.

"Odd? How odd?" asked Dottie, "Strange, ya mean, or …?"

"Well," Ruthie said, shifting her weight which was considerable, and putting her hands firmly on her knees, "well, you see, her family useta be, or at least they thought they was. Special, I mean. Her father made a heap a money in a mine Up North an' then, well, he just disappeared. The whole family disappeared. Dropped right outta sight. That was just after the bank noticed somethin' wrong with th'accounts." She sniffed again. "One a the sons worked there, you see. In the bank. An' folks thought as there musta been some kinda monkey bidness goin' on. Them disappearin' so close, like. The Oateses, that's the name. No one ever heard a thing about 'em till she suddenly come back. Just a few weeks ago, I heard tell."

Oates? Now where've I heard that name before? Aloud Dottie said, "What's so odd 'bout her?" She was dying of curiosity, but Ruthie hesitated again.

"Well, I dunno if I should say this, but, well … she dresses like someone from a coupla hunnert years ago. You know? Long skirts, hats, gloves up to here?" she pointed to her elbow. "Dya mind how some women useta rig themselves out? 'N this is all the time. Every day. Not just for goin' somewhere special, like dinner or somethin'."

Dottie didn't think her clothes would make her all that odd. After all, what *she* wore was a little different from most of the local women. There must be something else.

As if reading her thoughts, Ruthie's chair creaked ominously as she leaned against the back. "*And,* just wait till you hear *this!*"

Dottie had the biggest urge to put her hands over her ears. *I hates gossip, but better give a listen anyways. Ya never know...* She smiled at her visitor and resigned herself to the inevitable.

17
STRANGE LAKE

Rab woke up earlier than usual one morning and realized he hadn't been up to the farm property for some time. It had taken longer than expected to get the road unblocked, and he hadn't been able to be up there while that was going on. Then Smale's, the grocery in Bickerton, had had to close for almost two weeks 'DUE TO ILLNESS IN THE FAMILY', it said on the notice in the front window. But that wasn't the real reason. The boy who looked after the produce section let slip to his girlfriend he'd seen mice in the back storeroom. A whole bunch of them. As usual, the grapevine was in good working order and the news soon spread everywhere. This break had kept Rab busier than ever. His reputation for a good variety of merchandise was becoming well known in Bickerton and beyond. Never mind in East Tee. *Kinda tough on old Vic Smale, though, this bein' the tourist season an' all,* was Rab's first thought when he heard the news. But he was smart enough to know business was business and he bent over backwards to make sure his new, if only temporary, customers were satisfied.

No mice had shown their whiskers at *his* store. Not yet anyway. But it did set him to thinking he should get him a couple of cats. CeeCee had brought her cat with her, but Shadow was getting too old to care much about catching anything except forty winks. Which he did most of the time. At least, he was asleep every time Rab saw him. He'd have to ask the oldtimers if they knew who might have some kittens. Come to think on it, there were kittens up to Jim Arkell's place. Jesse had been playing with them up in the loft at Jim's barn. But not for long. He told Rab he was afraid of falling in love with one of them and he knew his mom couldn't have cats in the house. Made her wheeze, she said. She sure didn't need anything like that to upset her right now.

Jim had sent a message that his brother Aaron was coming down soon to talk to Rab about witching another well somewhere on the old farm. Maybe Aaron could be persuaded to drop by Jim's place on the way down and bring a couple of those kittens with him. Rab didn't know what Dottie would think, but then she hated mice or any sort of vermin, so he was sure she wouldn't say no.

The following Thursday midmorning, Aaron showed up in an old beater truck with **World's Greatest Water Finder** in faded lettering on the side. He had the same wide-set light brown eyes as his brother, but was half a head taller, and solemn-faced like the sister Dolly. He eased the truck around to the back of the store, reached over on the seat beside him and climbed out with a covered basket that was mewing pitifully.

"Didn't want the world to think you had water problems," was Aaron's reply when Rab asked why he hadn't used the parking lot. He was wearing heavy work boots, the kind with steel toes, and baggy pants held up by a length of rope and with knees that must have seen a lot of wear, they were so decorated with multi-coloured patches. He swiped at his face with the sleeve of his plaid flannel shirt, cleared his throat and spat. The distinct odour of tobacco rose up beside the truck.

"Sure turned out real hot for this early in the summer, eh?" he said, handing the basket to Rab who had just finished repainting the store sign he'd brought in from the roadside. "These little fellers'll take care of any mice. Just don't feed 'em too much, gotta keep 'em good and hungry if you wanna make 'em into hunters."

Rab said he didn't know about that, seeing as how both his sister and their house guest had such soft hearts when it came to animals. Especially baby ones. The kittens would probably be spoiled rotten. He took the noisy basket without lifting the top and carried it into the store. When he came back out, Aaron was sitting on the running board of his truck, rolling a cigarette.

"What's all this about needin' a well witched? Haven't you got enough water here?" was his question after he'd lit up and taken a couple of puffs. Rab stuck his wet brush he'd been using into an old coffee can of paint thinner and stood back to admire his handiwork which read **KIBBIDGES GENERAL STORE** in large green letters on a light blue background and underneath in much smaller ones *If we don't have it, you don't need it.* He explained to Aaron all about the farm and what he planned to do there. He was just about to give directions when Aaron said abruptly, "That's a mite far, you know. I stick pretty well to around here. Don't know as I'd wanna …"

Rab could see Aaron wasn't comfortable about leaving his own turf, so he said not to worry they'd be going up together as soon as the day's delivery of bread and cakes arrived from Dunhampton. It should have been here already, he said.

At the mention of cake, Aaron perked up. "Well," he said slowly, "guess that'll be okay by me. Not much else goin' on right now, any road." He took a couple of quick puffs and stubbed his cigarette out on the sole of his boot. "Where'd you say this place is at?"

Some time later, after having stopped for coffee to go with the raspberry jelly roll Rab had picked out of the bakery delivery, the two men found themselves at the newly bulldozed entrance to the old farm. Massive gray boulders, some with chunks of sod still clinging to them, were heaped up on either side.

"Road in is still mighty rough," Rab warned, as the truck started slowly up the lane. "Gotta get her levelled out some."

"Aw, my old bus here can handle anythin'," Aaron said as he skilfully avoided a series of gaping holes. Rab was pleasantly surprised to see how many of the trees in the small orchard had the beginnings of fruit on them, even though there'd been a fair bit of rain over the past few weeks.

"Looks like you got yourself some good old fruit trees up here. Apple, pear, maybe even cherry from the look a them," Aaron echoed his thoughts, as they approached the old weather-beaten house that had so fascinated CeeCee. After hoisting their gear from the back of the truck, they were starting up past the house when Aaron stopped short.

"Well, would you take a gander at that!" He pointed up ahead. "Looks like a lake, don't it?"

Rab looked and was amazed to see the field that stretched out behind the house was a sea of blue up as far as the distant row of trees. He couldn't remember having seen anything like it before. It did indeed look like a lake, shimmering in the freshening breeze that had sprung up since they left the truck, cooling the overwarm air.

"What the dickens *is* that stuff?" he asked as he bent down to take a closer look.

"Them? Why, they's Blue Devils. Leastways, that's what we call 'em. Devils they are, too. Will bite you if you try pickin' 'em. Full a sharp prickles, they are. Like a cactus. Good thing you ain't plannin' on havin' no lawn. Or are you? You'll have a devil of a time diggin' em out." Aaron snorted at his own wit and slapped his leg. "Broke my best knife cuttin' 'em outta our grass, but Allie, that's the wife, she hates the sight a them things. Says they bring bad luck, that's what her old pappy told her."

He hurried to catch up with Rab who was striding ahead, ignoring Aaron's comments. He didn't believe weeds could bring bad luck, but he was too polite to say so. And anyway, they were there to look for water, weren't they?

The day was getting warmer, in fact it was turning out downright hot. And humid. Even walking made the two men sweat. Aaron thought they'd better start by checking out the well, if that's what it was, that Buzzy had fallen into. After some probing, he could soon see what Rab had said about it was true. It appeared to be blocked good and solid by boulders about six feet down.

"Well now, I hate to say so but you got yourself a mite of a problem if you want to use that there well, Mr. Kibbidge," said Aaron, taking off his cap and scratching his head. Fishing a half-smoked cigarette from his shirt pocket, he struck a match with his thumbnail and lit up.

"The name's Rab. Don't hold with no fancy stuff." Rab was mentally kicking himself. They should have come here sooner. Today was really too hot to work.

Aaron took another good puff of his cigarette. "The guy what done that sure don't want no one to get at that water. And there's water down there, all right. I can smell it. Let's check up by them trees. It's a mite far away, but who knows? I found water in stranger places. Got me a feelin' we just might get lucky. Never mind them Blue Devils."

They waded up through the 'water' in the field of blue, glad they were wearing boots, up as far as the distant row of trees. Aaron forged ahead with his witching gear that consisted of no more than a bent coat hanger.

"You can find water with that?" Rab asked in surprise, pointing at the rusty piece of metal. "But I thought …"

"Yep. Sure. You can do it with a piece a hazel wood, but this here works just as good. Gotta have the feel for it, doncha know?"

As they continued to cross the 'lake', he went on to tell Rab he'd even been asked to witch a graveyard.

"What? Why would anyone wanna look for water there?" was Rab's startled response.

"No, no. Not water, never water. Seems they wasn't sure if any graves had been dug in an old section a the place. So they figured if I could witch it, that would tell 'em if there was any holler spots. Seems they're runnin' outta space."

Rab just shook his head at the thought of it and walked faster. He really didn't want to hear what Aaron might have found. In a graveyard of all places. When they finally reached the trees, he was startled to see that Aaron didn't stop there, but pushed through the lower branches and disappeared. Rab followed and was surprised to see a long pile of brush several feet beyond the trees. When he got closer, he could see what he'd thought was a brushpile was really a heap of dead trees lying in rows on top of each other.

"Got yourself a blow-down here. Yessirree, a blow-down." When he saw Rab looking puzzled, Aaron continued, "Yep, some strong wind come through here an' took all them cedars down. An' even took down them three big pines in the middle of 'em. An' where there's cedars, there's water. Place feels like it needs witchin'. I told you I can smell water. Even way under the ground. Let's just see now." Hooking the coat hanger through one of the belt loops on his pants, he began pulling the dead trees apart and dragging them away from each other. "Gimme a hand here, will you?"

Rab took a deep breath and bent to the task.

18
UNANSWERED QUESTION

Daffy Sturgeon was still jittery although no more scary letters had appeared in the mailbox at Saint Peeps. No more spooky calls on the church telephone either. She'd called Syd a couple of times, but he had no hard advice to give her, just that Constable Gussie was looking into it. But so far, nothing.

A week or so ago, she'd run into Dottie and CeeCee on Main Street as they were coming out of the Cosy Corner, wishing once again they hadn't eaten so much. Especially that coconut cream pie with the chocolate fudge sauce. Dottie stopped her as she was hurrying by and quick hellos-how-are-you-just-fine-thanks-and-you had been exchanged. When Dottie hesitated, CeeCee jumped in.

"Daffy, that is, we've been, that is, don't quite know how to say this but …"

"Is there somethin' goin' on with that minister fella, what's his name again?" Dottie couldn't wait for CeeCee to get to the point. "We bin singin' in the choir …"

"Yes, I've seen you there," Daffy said, wondering where this was going.

"Well," said Dottie, not looking Daffy in the eye, "we noticed, that is, CeeCee 'n me, we noticed th'other people in the choir act kinda funny when he's around. Not while we're singin'. The rest of the time. Has ya noticed?"

Daffy didn't know quite how to respond to this. Or even if she should. Would it be disloyal to the man she worked for? Or was it the church she worked for? Or both? She'd never been sure. It was true, what Dottie was saying, but she was surprised to hear it was obvious to anyone besides herself.

The new reverend was a bit strange, all right, popping into her office and then a few minutes later popping out again. Without saying a word. Maybe it was, what were they called again? Maybe he gave off what people were calling bad vibes. She thought it rather unusual that not one young couple had come in for marriage counselling. In fact, there hadn't been any weddings in the church since he came. That in itself wasn't normal. There were always those couples who'd been 'caught' and had to make a rush for the altar before the town started the gossip line going. 'Have you seen Jenny lately? Looks a bit off colour. Wonder if she's, you know …?' 'Heard Jerry hadda quit school and get a job Up North. His folks are real mad at him, him and that Carol girl.' 'Doesn't Sue, you know, the Beggs' girl, well, is she gettin' fat, or, I mean …?'

Deciding to take the easy road, Daffy mumbled something about have-get-to-an-appointment-see-you-soon, and hurried on. CeeCee and Dottie looked at each other, then continued walking back to where CeeCee had left her car.

"Guess we should have kept quiet, eh Dot? Was plain to see the girl didn't want to talk about it," CeeCee said, while Dottie said under her breath, "Humpf, we'll soon see 'bout *that!*"

19
RAB KEEPS MUM

After he and Aaron Arkell had been up to the farm, Rab was home late for dinner. That had never happened before and it started with Dottie worrying about him and ended with her throwing out the plate of food she'd saved for him. *Dried up to a crisp, only fit for the garbage pail, darn him anyway,* she muttered as she banged the lid of the pail as hard as she could. She hated to waste food, remembering only too well how little they'd had sometimes. Back Home. *Nothin' but beans. For weeks on end it seemed.* Just thinking about it, she squinched up her nose. She finished cleaning the kitchen counter. She refused to leave a mess for the morning. It always depressed her and besides it looked slummy. Aloud she said, "What happened to ya tonight? 'Bout given up seein' ya again in this world."

Rab was busy washing his hands at the sink and didn't respond right away. That was too much for Dottie who reached over and gave him a sharp tap on the backside.

"Have a heart, girl. I'm some bushed," he said as he dried his hands on one of her old aprons. "Nothin' to eat tonight, jest a cuppa yer good strong tea, there's me girl." He went over to the kitchen table and plumped himself down heavily on his usual chair. Taking a faded handkerchief out of his shirt pocket, he wiped his face and took a deep breath.

"Ya don't wanna know what kinda day I had, girl. No, ya don't. Now, howza 'bout that tea?" He didn't want to tell her Aaron said the whole place made him feel a bit strange. Or that they'd uncovered something troubling.

"Not till ya tell me what happened an' why yer so late in ta dinner." Dottie sat down opposite him. She was glad CeeCee was out tonight. Not there to see how brother and sister weren't getting along, a tall, a tall.

20
GUSSIE IS SWAMPED

Gussie was disgusted with herself. She hadn't made much progress on figuring out who was sending the nasty letters to Saint Peeps. More than likely they were aimed at the new reverend, but she needed proof. She knew perfectly well assumptions were unacceptable in police work. In fact, they were in the same category as gut feelings. *It's not what you know, it's what you can prove.* No, proof was definitely needed. But how to get it? None of the envelopes was postmarked and neither the envelopes nor their contents bore any trace of fingerprints other than Daffy's, who hadn't liked having her own prints taken. She said it made her feel like a criminal. Gussie assured her it was necessary to make sure they really were her prints. Whoever was writing and delivering the letters obviously knew enough to wear gloves.

The messages themselves were written on that lined canary-yellow paper, a favourite of lawyers and business people for making notes. Cheap stuff. Easily available anywhere stationery is sold. Same went for the envelopes. No help there. For all of them - so far - the messages were in a shade of purple, adding a touch of the weird to their appearance. Who the heck uses purple ink? She'd already checked at the stores in Bickerton and surrounding towns that carried office and school supplies. The yellow paper they stocked sure enough, but none carried purple ballpoints. Or purple ink. Nor had they ever done so.

Gussie turned her thinking to the reverend. If he was indeed the person referred to in the letters, did that mean he was in immediate danger? And should he be warned? But that might cause more of a problem than she knew how to handle. *Why is it people are so afraid to think their minister could be involved in anything shady? Aren't churchmen human beings like everyone else?*

While she was puzzling this out, the intercom chirped. Pressing the button, she heard Myrna the receptionist say in her breezy way, "Hey Gus, that little guy owns the grocery over to East Tee, you know? Cribbage or somethin'? He's on the phone. Wants to come in and see you. Sounded kinda urgent. Do you wanna talk to him or should I just …?"

"It's okay, Myrna, I'll take it." Gussie wondered what Rab Kibbidge was calling about. She hadn't forgotten what a help he'd been in finding the second body in the Denton case. Come to think on it, she hadn't seen much of him since. She pressed another button and said, "Hello there, Rab! And how've you been? Haven't seen you in ages. How's things?" She listened intently for a moment then said, "You better come over right after you close the store, when will that be? In another hour or so? Fine, I'll be waiting."

After hearing what Rab had to say that evening, Gussie's police sense swung into high alert. He'd shown up at her office, rather reluctantly she thought, and had to be asked twice to sit down. After the usual chitchat, he finally got around to the reason for his visit. Seems two days before, he and another man had gone up to the old farm Rab had bought a few weeks ago. They were on a water hunt, as the only well they could find on the place was blocked. Real bad feeling around that well, he said. The other man was supposed to be good at witching and did Gussie know what that was? She laughed and said she hadn't heard that word in ages and didn't they call them water diviners now? Or dowsers? Rab said well whatever they called it, this fella can do it all right. He went on to explain how they'd moved a huge pile of dead trees and brush and been shocked at what they'd uncovered. Bones. All kinds of them. And they looked like human bones. When she asked him why he thought that's what they were, he said some had bits of cloth stuck to them.

"All scattered 'round, like. Some looked as though they bin gnawed on. By animals." He paused. "No skulls though. Coulda bin carried off. Kinda gruesome, 'twere. Aaron, that's th'other guy, Aaron thought we should leave 'em alone an' talk to you, but …" He paused again.

"Oh, you did the right thing, I mean, the right thing," Gussie said quickly, trying to set the little man at ease. "But tell me, why did you wait till now? Why didn't you call me right away?"

"Well, Missus," Rab looked down at the floor. "Well, I didn't want to say anythin' too quick, like. Not being from round here. No idea who might be involved or …"

"At least you've told me now. You might better tell me where this place is at and I'll take a couple of fellows up there with me and have a little look-see, I mean, a look-see."

Rab frowned. " 'Twas my sister made me come. She was right mad at me for bein' so late home that night. She wouldn't make tea for me till I told her."

"Your sister is a wise woman, Rab. She understood what was going on in the Denton case better than anyone, I mean, than *anyone*. Good thing you listened to her." And she got out a map so Rab could show her where the farm was. While he was doing that, he was thinking of asking if he could go along. Dottie and Jesse could look after the store. And it was *his* farm, after all. But then he remembered how odd he'd felt that day and how ghastly the bones looked and decided against it.

After Rab had gone home to East Tee, Gussie was left wondering what to do next. That is, apart from dealing with the problems that arrived every year with the influx of tourists and the trouble they could get into. Rowdy parties late into the night. Drinking too much at the Snake Pit, the town's only bar. The odd bit of shoplifting. And apart from those nasty letters, nothing had happened lately to give her such a feeling of anticipation that she might have some real detective work to do. Maybe she could get a couple of auxiliaries down from Cooley's Mills to help her with this latest problem. This was one time she wasn't going to try to go it alone.

21
SYD IS DISAPPOINTED

The next morning, Gussie called up to the police detachment at Cooley's Mills to see if they had two auxiliaries they could spare for a special job which she would tell them about when they got there and no, she couldn't reveal the details. Not just yet. Just for the day, she said. And could they come real early, like five in the morning? And they needed to be big strong guys. The work could turn out to be heavy. And they should wear boots and be prepared to get dirty. Then she called Syd who was already in the newspaper office even though it was still early.

"Hey there, Gus, what's up? I can only talk for a minute. Some guy's coming in this morning to look over the shop. A prospect, I hope," he said with a wry laugh.

Gussie was quick to agree. She knew how much he wanted to get out of the newspaper business. It had been part of the reason why their marriage had failed. When she told him about Rab finding bones, Syd just snorted.

"Are you sure the guy hadn't hoisted a few? That sounds pretty wild to me. And where *is* this place anyway?"

"Oh I doubt that. Rab isn't a drinker, at least I don't think so. And anyway he wasn't anxious to tell me the story at all, I mean, at all. The old farm is up past the Lonesome a ways. I've already done some digging at the Town Hall. The records for that property are in a real mess, I mean, a real mess. No taxes have been paid on it for donkey's years and no one seems to remember too much about the last family that lived up there. At least, no one I've talked to so far. Maybe they just don't want to remember."

She sighed. "All I could find out was it was common knowledge, I mean, common knowledge the whole bunch of them had disappeared, no one is sure when." Another pause. "Oh yeah, and one of them was supposed to have been off his nut, I mean, off his nut. Do you think there might have been something in the *Bugler* about it? Could you look it up in your morgue? Isn't that what they call it, where you store copies of all the old papers? Such an awful name."

"Yeah, it *is* kind of grim-sounding," Syd said agreeably. "Um, come to think on it, I do remember Dad saying something about 'those darned hillbillies doing the vanishing act'. And something about no one daring to go up there, they were all crazy wild. Especially the one guy. I was just a kid when I overheard him telling Mom about it and I had no idea what a hillbilly was. When I asked him, Dad said they were people who didn't like anyone but themselves. I remember thinking that was kind of funny as I thought they were some kind of goat!"

They both burst out laughing and then Syd said, "Sure. I can do that before I go home tonight. See if Dad wrote it up, I mean. Hey, do you think I could come with you when you go up there? Might be a real good story in it."

Gussie took a second or two to answer him. "Oh, Syd, I don't know if that would be such a good idea. Not just now. I wouldn't want the thing to get out before I've had a chance to work on it a bit longer, I mean, a bit longer."

"Aw, com' on, Gus, please? Promise I won't write a word till you say so. Cross my heart."

"It's no good promising. I'd let you come if I could. You know that, I mean, you *know* that. Let me check the place out first."

Gussie knew she'd feel better with him along. She knew he'd keep his promise, but she didn't want to break any more rules than she had to. No need to get in trouble at this stage of the investigation. But bones? Probably just some old settler's grave. But then again, maybe not.

Two days later, when the auxiliaries from Cooley's showed up just after sunrise, Gussie had been hoping Perce would be one of them. Not much chance of that though. Several auxiliaries were needed up at the mill town as they had the whole area north of the town to look after. Not many people were living up there, not yet anyway, but still it was too large a territory for one man to cover. Perce had been such a big help to her during the investigation into the two strange deaths over that terrible never-ending winter. No such luck this time. No Perce. And no Butch either. Gussie guessed his wife had prevailed and he'd had to give up police work. Too bad. Both of them had been real good to have along and both had kept their mouths shut about what they'd seen. *Oh well, let's see who they sent down.*

After they'd introduced themselves, Gussie began to think these two might be even better for what she needed done. The taller one said his name was Mike and when he shook her hand, she was afraid he might break it, his grip was so firm. He towered over her and looked like a good 250 pounds of solid muscle. His eyes were a warm brown and his hair was black and cut very short on the sides, while his skin was a coppery bronze. Up to Cooley's, he said, he hauled scrap metal and clapped-out farm machinery. Cars and trucks too, he said. If he could get them.

The shorter one was built like the proverbial brick house, with hair that looked like a wildfire, bushy eyebrows to match, and startling green eyes in a broad sunburnt face. He said his name was Ivan, but to please call him Rusty. *Not at all surprising with that amazing hair.* His regular job was in general maintenance for the Upper Township. After shaking hands with Gussie - another bonecrusher - he told her Butch said to say hello. He was working full time in security at the mill now. Both men said they'd heard Perce had gone off to Police College. Last year. Always wanted to be a cop, they said.

"That's wonderful news, the best I've had in a long time! We sure could use more cops out here, so many new people moving in." Gussie was elated. She wondered if there was a chance if ... *just have to wait and see. Let's stick to the present, shall we?* Quickly she went on to welcome the two men. "Good to have you fellows aboard, you're just the ticket for this job" and she proceeded to tell them what she wanted.

22
DOTTIE ISN'T GIVING UP

After their encounter with the church secretary, Dottie was certain sure, more than ever sure, there was something fishy about the new minister. Why had Daffy been so unwilling to talk about him? Loyalty is one thing. But she seemed reluctant to say anything, even if it wasn't exactly the truth. Maybe it would be a good idea to make friends with the minister's wife, what was her name again? Wilbertina. Such an old-fashioned name. But wait. Hadn't she said to call her Bertie, that first Sunday? *Well, Bertie me girl, let's jes' see whacha has to say.*

During Fellowship Hour following the Sunday worship, while the church members who'd lingered were busy discussing their week's doings - a polite way of saying they were gossiping about whoever wasn't there - Dottie saw her chance to approach the minister's wife. Going into the kitchen where Bertie was washing up the coffee cups, Dottie grabbed a tea towel off the rack and joined her at the sink. A strong scent of lavender rose up from the woman as she swished the cups around in the soapy water and rinsed them under the tap.

"Oh hello, there. Dottie, isn't it? From over to East Thorne."

Before Dottie could respond, Bertie held up a cup. "Sure could use some new china, eh? Lookit this cup. Must be a hundred years old, it's so chipped."

"Noticed that myself. 'Taint healthy to use it. But I gotta warn ya. They near took off my head when I suggested they oughta think on gittin' some new stuff." Dottie grinned. "Everythin' in this here kitchen come from somebody's great aunt er grandmother er somethin'. Chipped china. Some's cracked too. Cream an' sugars with chunks outta the rims 'n missin' ther lids. Worn down forks. They say they can't get rid of nothin', somebody or other's feelins ull git hurt."

As she began to stack the dried cups and saucers on the shelf, Dottie couldn't help noticing the dress Bertie was wearing. It looked like pure silk. Silk? On a minister's salary? A deep midnight blue, it was sprigged with tiny pink rosebuds and had short, puffy sleeves edged with a frill of cream lace. Her plump arms were dimpled at the elbow and she was wearing a matching lacy apron to keep her dress from getting splashed. She must have been concentrating so hard on the washing-up that she jumped when Dottie said, "So where dya come from? Me 'n my brother now, we're from way Back East. Long way aways from here. Are ya local er what?"

Bertie ran some more hot water into the sink before replying, "Oh no, no, we've lived all over. Up North, way way up, and then the West Coast and then …" She was interrupted by CeeCee coming in to look for Dottie, who made a face at her behind Bertie's back and shook her head. Too late, CeeCee realized she'd blundered into something. She stood her ground though and said she wanted to remind Dottie they had company coming in for lunch and hadn't they better get on home. That gave Dottie an idea.

"Why doncha come on over to us fer lunch one day, say, next week? What's a good day for ya, Tuesday er Thursday? Does ya knit? CeeCee 'n me, we got us a nice little corner full a wool 'n needles 'n such."

Drying her hands on a towel, Bertie turned to face them. Her pale frizzy hair was dark with sweat and she wrinkled her small nose before saying, "Why, that's neighbourly of you! I'll have to check with Simon, but I think maybe Thursday would be all right. Is your phone number on the church registry? I can let you know."

Dottie wasn't anxious at this point to reveal that neither she nor CeeCee were members of the church, so she said quickly, "I'll save ya the bother. Got a scrap a paper on ya, CeeCee?"

On their way back home, CeeCee found herself getting really cross with Dottie, who was humming one of the hymns they'd sung that morning. Not taking her eyes off the road, she said, "What was *that* all about? What are you up to now? Don't you think …"

"No, I don't think. Goin' too far. That's whacha was goin' to say, weren't it?" Dottie shifted in her seat. She was glad to be getting home soon so she could get rid of her pantyhose. She sure hated getting dressed up. Too uncomfortable. Without pausing she retorted, "Any-the-hoo, what was *that* 'bout company for lunch? News to me, *that* were."

Crossing the bridge over the Canal, CeeCee realized she and Dottie were on the verge of a quarrel. That was the last thing she wanted. Maybe this *would* be a good way to find out what was going on with the new minister. Without raising any suspicions. If anyone could get something out of someone without them knowing it, it was Dottie.

23
THE BONEYARD

So far, everything was going smoothly. The sun was just starting a new day, mist was rising off the fields, and no rain was expected. The auxiliaries had been briefed on what they were expected to do. As Gussie requested, they were wearing overalls and heavy boots, but minus their police vests with **AUXILIARY** in big black letters on the bright yellow. Instead they sported royal blue T-shirts with *Cooley's Comets* in silvery letters on the front. Just before leaving, Gussie threw a few hard hats in the back of Syd's truck she'd borrowed at his suggestion to keep people from wondering where she might be going. She really wished she could have let him come. He had a true newsman's eye and might just pick up on something she'd miss.

The auxiliaries had come down in an unmarked truck with massive tires for difficult terrain which was good, as Syd's old truck had a tendency to get stuck if the going got tough. Still, Gussie thought it better they went up in separate vehicles. There might be an emergency she would have to get back home for. She slapped at her side pocket to make sure she had her beeper with her. She still wasn't used to the darned thing. But orders were orders. Her bosses in Dunhampton said she had to carry it with her at all times. She suspected up past the Lonesome she'd be out of range.

Before making any plans, she'd phoned Rab to see if he wanted come with them, but he said quickly, oh no, ma'am, I'm goin' nowheres near the place till you figure out what's what an' that boneyard's gone. She was a bit surprised at his reaction. She'd never taken him to be superstitious.

Just shows you never can tell about people. He gave her specific instructions on how to find the farm. Said he forgot to mention an old sign he'd seen lying in the ditch before the turnoff to the sideroad. It was badly worn but you could still make out what it said – **SLACKERVILLE – POP. 31.** When she told Syd about it, he almost shouted at her that yes, he'd heard that name before. He still hadn't had time to check the old records stored under the stairs in the Town Hall and was still struggling with the *Bugler* morgue. Not easy to figure out from his dad's way of filing things. But having a name to go on was a great start.

They'd driven several miles before Mike realized the usually chatty Rusty hadn't said a word and seemed a bit edgy. He couldn't possibly be nervous about the job they were going to do. Or was he? Mike was puzzled at his behaviour. They'd worked together lots of times before, but he'd never seen Rusty act like this. Finally, Mike broke the silence.

"Hey, buddy, what's eating you this morning? Did you have a fight with your wife last night?" he asked jokingly, knowing the guy had a temper that was easily set off at the mention of Josie.

"I don't know," Rusty said slowly, "don't know about working for a woman. I mean, look at her. Too good looking for police work, wouldn't you say? How do you think she'd …"

"Hey, buddy, haven't you heard? About Gorgeous Gussie and the Watson twins? No? Oh, I forgot. You were still Up North when that happened. Well, I don't want to get into it now. I'll tell you on the way home tonight. You'll be surprised."

An hour or so later, the little convoy pulled in at the newly bulldozed entrance to the farm. The sign for the long-gone Slackerville had been in the ditch where Rab said it was. Rusty told Mike he didn't know this road, had never been in here. He didn't think it was even on the map. Funny though, it being in the Upper Township where he thought he knew all the roads. Later, he told Gussie he'd check it out when he got back up to Cooley's. They still had all the old maps of the area, he said.

By now, the sun was much higher in the sky. When they climbed out of their trucks, the three of them realized it was going to be a really hot and humid day, the kind that seems to hit without warning in early summer in Southern Ontario. Especially the humidity part. They'd driven in as far as they could and now had to lug their gear up behind the house. Gussie was glad Syd's old bus hadn't overheated as it had a tendency to do.

It was the silence that got to her first. The only sound was a slight rustling of leaves in a couple of scraggly poplars that, from the jagged stumps on either side of them, were the only ones left of a row that had once edged the newly reopened lane. But she knew poplar leaves move in the lightest of breezes. Still, there was a feeling of sadness, of desertion, of dread even, in the air. She wondered if the others were aware of it. But neither gave any indication of something being out of the ordinary. She made a mental note to ask Dottie and CeeCee if they'd noticed anything. She didn't want to ask Rab. He might be upset if he thought he'd bought a place that made people uneasy.

As they passed the old house – Mike saying he wondered how long it had been since anyone had lived there, and Rusty remarking he didn't really care as it gave him the creeps – they stopped suddenly, as Rab and Aaron had done, and gazed at the sea of blue stretching out before them.

"Good thing we all wore high boots," was Mike's first comment. "Wouldn't want to get mixed up with that stuff."

"Means bad luck, I heard. From my grandaddy. This here's the biggest spread of Blue Devils I've ever seen. And I've seen plenty." Rusty shifted the weight of his gear and started making his way through the blue.

More superstitious stuff. Never heard that one before. Rab hadn't said a word to Gussie about any Blue Devils. Was he afraid if she knew about them, she wouldn't want to explore the area? Just showed he didn't know her very well. It would take more than a couple hundred spiky plants to throw her off, once she set out to do something. After all, deep snow hadn't stopped her from looking for the body in the woods, had it?

It was definitely getting warmer now and the two men's faces were shining with sweat before they got up as far as the old well. Gussie realized the sides had been built up above the ground with rocks, making it look like a crater on the moon. Rusty dropped his gear and bent over to take a closer look. Without warning, he boosted himself over the edge, dropped down into the well and disappeared.

"Hey there, Rusty, what the heck?" Startled, Gussie moved quickly to peer over the edge. *Gee, the guy took a chance, doing that. Good thing it was blocked or we would have had a problem straight off.*

"Your informant was right, it *is* only the height of a man. A bit taller man than I am, though. Should have let you try it, Mike," he said, as he hauled himself out again. "Blocked solid. Just like you said. Nothing moved, even with my weight landing on it. Lots of junk on top - rotten leaves and twigs - but if we can get a purchase on those boulders, we should be able to clear it okay. Lucky there's a couple of big trees close by. We can rig up that block and tackle we brought and get 'em out that way."

While Mike hiked back to the truck for a couple of thermoses of coffee, Rusty took an axe and a crowbar and started chopping down the sides of the well opening to make it larger. Gussie stood watching for a moment, then turned and began working her way up to where Rab and Aaron had moved the blown down trees. She couldn't stand it a minute longer, she just had to know whether there was a grave under them or not.

The land rose gently up to a kind of ridge, not too steep a slope to climb. It seemed to her quite a long way from the house to witch for a new well, but then Rab wasn't likely to live in that old wreck of a place. Or even want to stay there overnight. He'd build a nice new place somewhere else on the property. Wells can be sunk farther from the house as long as the water can be pumped to it, she remembered Mac telling her years ago. And surely Rab would get the power lines brought in and put in an electric pump. That is, if the lines were at all accessible. No point in taking a step backwards and trying to live the way folks did a hundred years ago, with one of those old hand-operated pumps and a bucket. He must have checked before he made an offer on the place to see just how far from the property the main power lines ran. Rusty might know, being in maintenance for the Upper Township. If he didn't, he'd probably know who did.

She was in the middle of shifting the smaller of the downed trees when a shout from below made her hurry back down to the old well site. Her curiosity would have to wait.

"Hey, Missus, we're ready to give her a go, okay?" Rusty called over his shoulder as he grasped the rope strung up over his head. Mike was out of sight. Probably in the well, fastening a sling around one of the rocks. At least, that's what it looked like to Gussie. She could only hope they knew what they were doing.

"That was real quick, I mean, real quick!" she said, trying to catch her breath. "And it's Gussie, please. Call me Gussie."

Mike popped out of the well, joined Rusty on the rope and shouted, "Haul away!"

Driving back down to Bickerton later that day, Gussie was glad she was alone in the truck. It would give her some time to think about what they'd found and what she'd have to do next. Below the boulders they'd found one of those heavy sewer covers you'd see in the City held up by a gridwork of metal bars. The cover they'd managed to haul out, but the bars were firmly cemented in place. They'd have to come back with more equipment and get those out before they could see down to the water. If there was any.

She rolled down both windows, hoping the breeze would cool her off. When they'd tramped back through the blue field, Mike commented it was too bad it wasn't a real lake. He could sure use a swim. Rusty only grunted and walked faster. On the way back up to Cooley's, he told Mike the quicker he could get away from those spooky Blue Devils, the better.

Under the fallen trees, once she'd hauled them out of the way, Gussie found a shallow depression where bones lay strewn about, just as Rab had said. No sign of a skull though. In the back of Syd's truck was a gunny sack full of all the bones she'd been able to find. She'd also collected some fragments of fabric that began disintegrating when she carefully slipped them into an envelope. Boneyard it was indeed, but whether it was a settler's gravesite or something else was hard to say at this point.

24
DOTTIE CONTINUES HER CAMPAIGN

Promptly at noon on the Thursday following Dottie's invitation to the minister's wife, Bertie Essery showed up at Kibbidge's little grocery in East Tee. Dressed as if she were going to a fancy restaurant, in a cornflower blue and white striped long-sleeved dress with French cuffs, and a triple strand of pearls around her pudgy neck, she teetered through the shop on lipstick-red spike-heeled shoes. Her matching red leather clutch purse was shaped like a heart. As CeeCee remarked to Dottie later on, those shoes alone would cost some folks a week's pay. Never mind the purse. And what about her perfume? The distinctive scent of Chanel No. 5 rose in a cloud around her. And that stuff wasn't cheap either.

Even though Bertie was quite plain, with colourless over-permed hair and pasty skin that looked as though it had seen its share of pimples, CeeCee couldn't help envying her style. The way she carried herself, she seemed so self-assured, something CeeCee herself had never been. After Hink's death, she'd gotten rid of a lot of the fancier clothes she'd brought from the city and bought new outfits more suitable to her reduced status. Although she didn't think of it as reduced. Just different. She envied Dottie too, but for an entirely different reason. Dottie didn't care a rap for fashion, as she'd said so often, but wore just exactly what she pleased, not caring whether it was outlandish or not. Today her choice was an old short-sleeved pale green cotton dress with black and white sheep and orange flowers sprinkled all over it. Maybe not so outlandish, but she'd added an orange baseball cap on top of her hair which was tied back with a matching ribbon that hung down to her waist. CeeCee was content in her simple blue seersucker shirtwaist dress. And comfortable. Which was more important.

After a lunch of golden brown corn fritters with maple syrup, crisp bacon, and an apple and carrot salad, served out on the porch, CeeCee excused herself to go back into the kitchen for the dessert. While she was gone, Dottie settled back in her chair and carefully organized in her mind what she wanted to say. So far, the conversation had been about cooking and meals and what was in season and where you could get it the cheapest. Now it was time to get down to business.

"My, that was a tasty spread," said Bertie, fanning herself with a linen hanky she took out of her sleeve. "Do you eat like that every day?" Her small birdlike eyes were darting here and there, landing everywhere except on Dottie's face. Dottie could see she hadn't made up her mind what kind of people they were.

"Oh, 'tisn't *all* we're gonna have," Dottie replied brightly, " 'twas only the first course. CeeCee's bringin' out the rest in a minnit. After that, we'll give ya a tour a the shop." She leaned forward. "Back on Sunday there, ya was tellin' me 'bout where all ya lived before ya come to Saint Peeps. Funny name for a church, eh? Kinda cute in a way. But that's what the locals've called it. For years now, they tell me."

Bertie cleared her throat before replying. "Uh, well, we've lived all over the countryside. The church never lets us get too settled anywhere. They like to move us every couple of years or so. I'm starting to lose track of some of the places, we were there for such a short time. Why do you ask?"

Dottie smiled to put her visitor at ease. "Don't mind me none. Just curious, I guess. Rab 'n me, we've only ever lived the two places – Cod Cove 'n here. What's it like ta move so much? It must be hard on ya."

"Well, uh, it *was* hard at first. For me, anyway. But I'm used to it now. We never really unpack all the way, only the basic things we need. The part that's still hard for me is I just nicely get to know the ladies and then it's on to the next place." She sighed. "I do hope I've got room for that, it looks delicious," she said, as CeeCee reappeared with a cut glass bowl of peach cobbler and a pitcher of vanilla sauce, setting them down carefully in front of Dottie and going back for the tea things. "Uh, do you two ladies share the cooking or …?"

"Oh dear no, it's all me," said Dottie cheerfully. "CeeCee never took ta cookin', she tells me. 'Twas her husband what did it all. When he was alive, that is." Inwardly she cringed as she realized that subject should not have been mentioned.

"What happened to him? If you don't mind me asking." Now it was Bertie's turn to be curious, but Dottie began doling out the cobbler and hoped she didn't have to answer.

She was saved when CeeCee put the tea tray on a side table and sat down to enjoy her dessert.

Lunch was over and after Dottie agreed to share the secret of why her cobbler was so light, Bertie said oh my, lookit the time. All three women stood up at once. There was a plop and Dottie looked down to see Bertie's pretty purse on the floor, its contents scattered under the table.

"I'm so sorry." Bertie was flustered as she bent down to collect her belongings. "So careless of me. I forgot it was on my lap."

"That's okay, don't give it another thought," Dottie said, as she got down on her knees to help. *Well now, would ya lookit that, that's a bit odd.* She stood up and handed Bertie the things she'd picked up. "Com'on, we'll show ya 'round the Knittin' Bin before ya go. Did ya say ya knit? Or was it rughookin' ya does?"

That night, as she and CeeCee were finishing up the dinner dishes, Dottie said in a whisper, "Ya'd never guess what that woman had in 'er purse. I couldn't hardly b'lieve my eyes."

"What's with the whispering? Rab's not here." Rab had taken Jesse back over to Bickerton a day early. His father was due home and both parents wanted to see him. "Is there someone else here I don't know about?" CeeCee found herself getting peeved. Her friend had been acting strangely since the lunch with the minister's wife. Oh, she'd been happy enough when Bertie bought enough yarn to make a cardigan. And a pattern and needles to make it with. But ever since the woman left, she'd been very quiet. CeeCee guessed whatever was bothering her, she just couldn't keep to herself any longer.

"Uh, well," Dottie began in a more normal voice, "before I tell ya, ya gotta promise me not ta breathe a word … "

"A word about what, Dottie? You've been acting funny since our visitor left. Out with it. What did she have in her purse anyway?"

Dottie put down her dishmop. "Ya mind when she dropped it? That cute little purse, I mean. And all the stuff went flyin' under the table? Well, when I got down ta help I saw a pack of what looked like cigarettes …"

"So she smokes. So what's wrong with that? Lots of women do." Now CeeCee's attention was fully caught. "Go on."

"Well, ya see," Dottie grasped CeeCee by the arm. "Well, the top a the pack'd burst open and what was stickin' out didn't look like no cigarettes I ever saw. Looked more like that stuff, ya know, what ya roll yerself 'n is against the law?"

"Pot, you mean? Marijuana? But Dottie …"

"Yeah, I know. She's a minister's wife 'n ministers' wives don't do things like that. Or does they?"

"Doesn't seem likely to me. What made you think it was pot?"

"Why, the powerful stink of it, natcherly. We had trouble with that stuff Back Home. Fella next door got caught with it. Was smokin' it out back in his shed 'n I was walkin' past one night 'n got a good whiff. Didn't know what it was till then. But someone musta tole on 'im 'n it all came out. That stuff outta her purse stunk just the same." She paused. "An' maybe that's why they has to move so often. So as not ta git found out. Come ta think on it, that's pro'ly why she dumps that whaddayacallit Channel stuff on herself. Kills the stink!"

"Are you going to do anything? I mean, report it? To Gussie?" was CeeCee's first thought.

"Mm, I got ta thinkin' on it. Could be that's where she gets the money for all them fancy duds."

"You don't mean she's a dealer? Oh Dottie! Don't think anyone would believe that! Anyway, you'd have to prove it. Wouldn't you?" CeeCee was shocked.

"Maybe I don't. Maybe I jest needa tell Constable Gussie what I saw 'n let her handle it. She's the cop lady, not me."

25
MONDAY MORNING BLUES

Cradling Buzzy in his arms, Jesse came back to Kibbidges' with Rab early on Monday. Normally he would have come bounding into the kitchen, delighted at being there again. But this morning was different. A glance at his face told CeeCee things weren't too good this Monday morning. He didn't seem to see her or Dottie, but went straight into his room and sat on the edge of the bed, still cuddling the pup who was licking the boy's face enthusiastically. Suddenly realizing he was late for breakfast, he put the pup down on his mat, told him to stay, and went out, closing the door. Back in the kitchen, he washed his hands at the sink and then sank into his chair with a glum look on his face. When he saw the others were waiting for him, he murmured, "Sorry I'm late." Then he startled them by announcing loudly, "Pop's back!"

"That's good news, Jesse," CeeCee said. "Know you weren't happy about your mother being there alone."

"Not so good news," Jesse said, in a voice barely above a whisper. "Doc Blair doesn't like the look of Mom. He's puttin' her in the hospital. Over to Dunhampton. Just to be on the safe side, he said. And anyways, Pop won't be home for long. A week, maybe. Or two." He bit his lip.

"Not to worry, Jesse. They'll take good care of her over there, I'm sure of it," CeeCee said, trying to reassure him.

"Um, don't know if I can eat this morning, Miz Kibbidge, um, not really hungry," Jesse said, looking at Dottie.

"Well that's okay, Jess, if that's the way ya feel," Dottie said, "I made buttermilk pancakes this mornin'. Ya know? Them ones ya liked so much when we had 'em before? But I guess if …"

"If the kid don't want 'em, I'd sure be glad of a taste," Rab said, "bring 'em on. Gotta get goin'. Monday's the busiest day, doncha know, after bein' closed all yesterday."

When the platter of steaming pancakes arrived, with slices of sugar-cured ham on the side, Jesse hesitated. "Well," he said slowly, "guess I could give it a try."

"That's the way, young fella. Got any mustard for this here ham, Dot?" Rab was busy slathering his share of the cakes with a mixture of butter and maple sugar. "Gonna need all yer strength today, me son. Got a big order a canned goods comin' in soon that'll need unpackin' 'n shelvin'." Rab was wise enough to know there's no substitute for work to take your mind off what's troubling you.

After Rab disappeared into the store and Jesse had gone to feed the pup and put him outside in his new pen, the two women lingered over their coffee. Both of them were delaying the start of a new work week. Dottie hadn't slept well the night before. Unusual for her. But she couldn't get the sight of those 'cigarettes' out of her head. And what they might mean.

CeeCee had been out with Gene again, this time for a drive into the City for the day. Gene wanted her to see a special exhibition of new furniture. She thought he was moving a little too fast for her when he insisted she try out a few of the chairs and sofas. And give him her opinion. Some of them were ridiculously expensive and upholstered in sleek black leather and shiny chrome. Secretly she thought they would look great in a nightclub. But in a house? She much preferred something like what she'd had in her old place – sofa and chairs covered in a rich plushy velvet. She hadn't known what to say to him, he was so enthusiastic, so she just smiled. On the way home, they'd stopped for dinner at a new seafood place in Dunhampton and he'd brought her home later than usual.

After a few minutes, CeeCee got up to refill her mug from the coffee pot on the stove. When she sat down again, she said, "What do you suppose is wrong with Kitty? Obviously they didn't tell the kid what's going on with her. Shouldn't they have?" She poured a dollop of cream into her coffee and stared down at it, thinking how pleasant it was to sit and inhale the aroma of her favourite brew. After they'd retired, Hink hadn't allowed her to drink the stuff. Said it wasn't good for her. Said tea was better. But she'd never really liked tea first thing in the morning. Especially the green stuff. Didn't energize her to do what had to be done. Not like coffee.

Dottie drained her own mug before replying, shaking her head when CeeCee asked her if she wanted a refill. "Could be Kitty's comin' close ta losin' the baby, lovey. She'll have to stay real quiet fer a good while 'n see if everythin' settles down. I mind the time when my mam …"

CeeCee sat up straighter in her chair. "Didn't Jesse tell you? Doc Blair thinks it might be twins!"

If Dottie had still been drinking her coffee, she might have choked. "Oh, my dear goodness! No, lovey, he didn't! He never said a word. No wonder he's worried! He told me one night he's wanted a brother for ages. 'Twill be a cryin' shame if anythin' happens now."

26
MORE BAD NEWS

The day after the excursion to the old farm, Gussie had been busy since early morning. The sack of bones was ready to be shipped off to a lab in the City to see if anything could be discovered about them. From what she'd read, the specialists could tell you almost anything from examining bones. How old they were. How long they'd been exposed to the weather. Even the approximate age the person had been. As soon as she thought Rab Kibbidge might be up, she'd phoned the store to tell him what had been done so far. She assured him the bones he'd found were gone. She told him the rocks were out of the well, but there was still lots more to be done. He was mildly surprised when she told him about the sewer lid and the heavy iron grid under the rocks. But there was one other discovery she held back on. She didn't want to put another scare into him.

Rab's thanks still ringing in her ears, she put in a call to Syd. She'd tried to get him earlier, but Myrna told her there was a barn fire over on the 10th Concession he'd gone out to check on. This time, he didn't call her back for close to an hour. When he did, his voice was solemn-sounding.

"Bad news, Gus. From up to Wildwood. They couldn't get a hold of you so they called me. Mac's been taken bad. Another heart attack. Can you get away so we can go up and see what's what?"

Gussie said oh my God wonder how bad it is and yes they should go but she'd have to let him know when. Myrna told her the only problem from the day before was a woman who'd reported her teenaged daughter Marcie hadn't come home from her summer job down at the new marina.

When Myrna questioned the woman, a Mrs. Hilling, she admitted it wasn't the first time the girl hadn't come home. She also said she'd had a fight with her daughter before she disappeared. At that point, the girl hadn't been missing for forty-eight hours, and as it turned out later, she'd stayed at a girlfriend's house and had told the friend's mother her parents knew where she was. Gussie sighed. *That one's disappeared before. One of these days she'll take off for good and end up lost forever in the City. Like so many others before her.*

On her way out the door, Gussie was surprised to see Dottie Kibbidge getting out of CeeCee Denton's car.

"Oh hello, Dottie. And CeeCee. Sorry. I can't see you now, I mean, not now. Dad's not so good again and I have to get up to Wildwood right away." And she climbed into Syd's old truck, which she still had, to get over to the *Bugler* office and pick him up. She vaguely wondered how he'd gotten up to the fire. She was cross with herself for forgetting about the message Myrna had left on her desk that Dottie Kibbidge wanted to talk to her. Syd's news had put it right out of her head.

Dottie and CeeCee said that's okay we understand family comes first maybe tomorrow. Gussie waved and was gone in a swirl of dust. They looked at each other and then CeeCee said, "Well, Dot, let's not make it a wasted trip, eh? How about some of that coconut cream pie at the Cosy Corner?"

27
TOUCH AND GO

In spite of the uncertain sound of the old truck's engine, Syd and Gussie made it up to Wildwood in record time. Gussie figured it was because it was too early in the week for tourists to be on the road. After they'd been rumbling along for a while, Syd said, "I swear to you, Gus, when – and you'll notice I said *when* not *if* – *when* I sell the *Bugler*, the first thing I'm going to do is buy a newer truck."

Gussie didn't respond right away. She turned slightly in her seat so she could look at him. As far as she was concerned, he was still the best looking guy around. And the nicest. For the millionth time, she cursed the day they'd split up. And all because of his worries over the darned *Bugler* and her stupid habit of repeating herself, which he couldn't take any more. Before she turned to face the road again, she said, "Well, I'd sure have mixed feelings about saying goodbye to this old bus. I feel kinda sentimental about it, I mean, sentimental. About the rips in the seats and the crazy door latch. I'd hate to lose those."

Syd murmured something under his breath and then said, "But, darling, we haven't lost each other yet. Have we? Do you think …?"

Gussie stopped him before he could go on. "I really don't think this is the time or the place to get into that now. First we've got to see what's going on with Dad, eh?" Syd didn't say a word but concentrated on driving. He was kicking himself for having brought up the subject. *Poor timing, you dope.*

After looking in on Mac, who was in an oxygen tent, his eyes closed and unaware of their presence, they had a quick conference with the doctor in charge. He told them Mac's situation was precarious as far as his heart was concerned. Everything possible was being done for him, but it would be touch and go for a few days. He promised to call if there was any real change. In the meantime, there was nothing for them to do but go home.

On the way back down to Bickerton, to take her mind off her father, Gussie told Syd as much as she could about the two auxiliaries and the boneyard. And about starting to unblock the well. But she didn't drop a hint about what she was afraid might be in it. She did say she thought he should come up with her the next time. The doctor would have to come with them, that is, if she could get a hold of him. Syd frowned at this, but renewed his promise not to print a word until she gave him the go-ahead. And then they decided to go back to her place and talk.

It was touch and go with Kitty Woodcock too. Albie was the only one who knew about it. Doc Blair said she would have to stay in the hospital until the babies were born. A little problem with the placenta, he said. When Albie asked him what he should do about Jesse, the doctor said it would be better if the kid didn't know about it. Not yet anyway. Albie was glad they'd decided to let Jesse work for the Kibbidges. That way he wouldn't be alone. Albie figured the case he was working on would allow him to come home for the odd weekend. What he was going to do when school started again, he didn't have a clue.

28
A CURIOSITY

CeeCee and Dottie were sitting in the Cosy Corner enjoying some pie and coffee, when Bertie Essery appeared at their table. CeeCee had been thinking Gussie must have been really upset over her father to take off like that, especially when she'd been told they were coming, while Dottie toyed with her pie, wishing Jennie Brant was still here baking her treats. This piece of pie had a tough crust, something Jennie's pastry had never had. Hers literally melted in your mouth.

"What a surprise to find you two here!" was Bertie's opening remark. A cloud of rosewater scent accompanied her. "Mind if I join you? Dottie, you promised to let me in on the secret of that fabulous cobbler of yours. Could I get the recipe from you now or do you remember it?"

Dottie took her purse off the third chair and said nice to see ya, go ahead, take a pew. CeeCee smiled inwardly when she heard that. Imagine saying 'take a pew' to a minister's wife! Dottie was always surprising her. Her own purse she'd slung by its strap over her knee, city style. Probably quite safe here in the country, but you never know who might be light fingered. She couldn't understand why people out here didn't lock up their cars. Who'd want this old heap, they'd said when she inquired. If they want it, they're welcome to it. A totally different attitude to a city person's. But she didn't like nasty surprises. Like the surprise of finding someone in the back seat of your car. Or worse.

After she'd ordered a piece of butter pecan pie and a mint tea, Bertie got out a pad and pen from her purse, a big powder blue satchel this time.

Dottie said, sure, I never forgit a recipe once I makes it a coupla times. As she began giving Bertie the directions, CeeCee found herself fascinated by Bertie's pen. It was as thick as man's thumb, and a silver colour, and studded with glittery stones that looked like amethysts. She looked down at the table to watch Bertie using it and saw that the writing was a rich shade of purple. A colour of ink she'd never seen used before. Green yes. But never purple. She wondered where Bertie had gotten such a pen and how easy it was to write with. It looked as if it would be hard on the fingers with all those bumpy stones sticking out. She didn't say anything but finished off the last forkfuls of her pie. Gene was picking her up again tonight. *Wonder where he wants to go this time? Wonder what I should wear? Oh dear, this is getting to be a bit of a problem. But I have to admit I'm having fun. Don't think I ever had so much fun before.* Occupied with her own thoughts, she stopped paying attention to what the other two were doing.

29
HEART TO HEART

After checking with their respective offices, leaving messages as to their whereabouts, and a quick supper of warmed-over beef stew and brown bread, Gussie and Syd stayed sitting at the table in her tiny kitchen, steaming mugs of coffee in front of them, a bowl of sweet black cherries and a plate of Dad's Oatmeal Cookies to share. No candlelight and wine for them. They wanted to keep the romantic stuff until after they'd had a chance to talk.

It was turning out to be a rough night. A thunderstorm was approaching. They'd seen the lightning flashing intermittently off to the northwest on the way down from Wildwood and heard a faint mutter or two of thunder. But, even though the atmosphere was supercharged, even if the heavens fell, they were determined to talk over their situation.

As the sky darkened and the rumbling thunder moved closer, Syd told Gussie the prospective purchaser of the *Bugler* was someone with newspaper experience who wanted to retreat to the slower pace of a small town. His job in the City had worn him down to a frazzle, he said. Slower it may have appeared, but Syd wasn't going to disillusion him on that score. For his part, he would love something even slower. And with regular hours. He didn't know what it might be yet, but he'd need some time to figure that out after the millstone *Bugler* was no longer hanging around his neck. The prospect wanted him to stay on for a while until the new ownership was well established in the minds of the townsfolk. Syd thought that might work, but was keeping an open mind.

The thunder was booming more frequently as Gussie told Syd she knew she'd been promising to put the pressure on the bigwigs over in Dunhampton to loosen the purse strings and get her a deputy, but hadn't gotten around to it. Bickerton had grown a lot since she first took on the policing job. And, as a matter of fact, so had East Thorne. Syd agreed with her on both counts. He said he'd noticed more and more escapees from the City taking up the abandoned farms and the smaller country properties. So the policing job, as well as the newspaper, covered more people within their bounds. Gussie said she was determined if this thing was going to work between them, she'd have to take action. Again Syd agreed.

The conversation shifted to Gussie's dad. With Mac so sick, there wasn't much chance of him coming back to live on his own in Bickerton, so Gussie said maybe she should rent out his house and use the money to put him into a really good nursing home. That is, once he'd served his time. Syd said what a good suggestion and well, he wouldn't have his dad's house any more once the paper was sold, so they'd have to look for someplace else to live. Gussie said for sure they could use more space as her apartment was far too cramped for two. They sat quietly for a few minutes, finishing off their coffee and listening to the storm move ever closer.

After they'd had their heart-to-heart, both were feeling better about things. They'd finally faced up to the fact they missed each other, more than either of them had wanted to admit. That they were still very much in love was obvious, but they both knew a lot of work would have to be done if they were to try living together again. No question about it. The first thing they'd have to do would be to change their over-demanding work situations. Somehow. The first time around, neither had had time for the other and both were exhausted when they did manage to be together.

"That, and me being stupid over your habit of repeating …"

"Shh!" Gussie cut through the sound of the rain on the roof. "No more talk about that. It was just as much my fault as yours, I mean, my fault as yours. Oh darn, there I go again!"

They were reaching across the table to clasp hands when there was a tremendous crack of thunder right over their heads and the lights went out.

"Well," said Syd, as they found themselves sitting in pitch dark, "guess we're going to need that candlelight after all!"

30
2 + 2 = ?

The next morning was damp and foggy. The rain was holding off, but the sky was heavy with the promise of more to come. Gussie dragged herself off to work with a pounding head. *Why, oh why, did we open that bottle of wine last night? And then polish off the whole thing? We must have been nuts. Oh well, at least we know where we stand so I guess it was worth it. Hope Syd feels the same.*

No sooner was she in the office than a call from Dottie Kibbidge came through. Gussie picked up the phone and said quickly, "Sorry I couldn't see you yesterday. Yes, thanks for asking, Dad's still very ill, but there's nothing to be done, I mean, nothing to be done. Yes, I hope he makes it but the doctor was doubtful, at least, that's the feeling I got. And Syd did too. We'll just have to wait and see. Can you make it over later today, say around four? You can? Good. I'll see you then. Bye now."

Hope I didn't sound too distant, but I can't afford to get distracted now. What could be so important that those two women are so all-fired anxious to see me about? Could it have something to do with the old farm? Can't think what else it could be. Guess I'll just have to wait and see.

Four o'clock came and went. It wasn't until after four-thirty that Gussie heard voices down the hall and Myrna buzzed her to say, those two ladies are back again, can you see them now? Gussie, who'd been buried in long overdue paperwork, was startled. She was surprised to see she'd completely lost track of time.

"Yes, yes. By all means. And Myrna, you can leave as soon as Jordy gets here." Jordy was the new night clerk sent over by Head Office. *Well, if they could afford another clerk, they could afford a deputy. I'll get on their case first thing tomorrow.*

When Dottie and CeeCee came into her office, they brought with them the smell of freshly washed streets. They draped their raincoats over the straight-backed chairs provided for visitors and sat down. After hello-again-how-are-you-sorry-we're-late-yes-it's-raining-again, there was silence. CeeCee sat staring straight ahead while Dottie looked around the room, her eyes wide. She took in Gussie's certificate next to the filing cabinet, the pale green walls decorated with **WANTED** posters, the pile of papers and folders on the cluttered desk. *She must have a heap a work, seein' all that mess a papers 'n such. I'd sure hate to be her, just hate paperwork.*

Gussie leaned forward in her chair. "Now, how can I help you?" Intensely curious as to why they were there, she waited patiently to hear what they had to say. She wasn't going to mention the old farm unless they did.

CeeCee said, "Dottie, *you* tell. It's your story after all."

Dottie looked down at her hands before replying. "We-e-ll," she began, "well, 'tis like this. Ya see, we ast her over ta lunch 'cause I was bein' nosey, 'tis all. Nosey, I was." She hesitated. "I best start again. Ya see, we invited the minister's wife, Bertie's her name, over ta our place last Thursday fer lunch 'n well, we was a mite shocked."

"Shocked? We were stunned!" CeeCee broke in.

"Am I gonna tell the story or …?"

"Sorry, Dottie, my fault, it's just that …"

Gussie smiled at the two of them. "Take your time now, Dottie. No need to rush, I mean, to rush. You invited the new minister's wife, Mrs. Essery, for lunch and …?" *What in heck was this all about?*

"Well, ya see, when she was leavin', she went 'n dropped that fancy purse a hers 'n everthin' fell out 'n, uh, well, I saw a package a, uh, a package a …"

Not understanding what was wrong with Dottie who was usually quick to speak, CeeCee couldn't stand it any longer. "A package of what looked like cigarettes," she said in a loud voice.

Dottie glared at her. "Why dya keep buttin' in? Ya know I never seen th'inside of a p'lice office before. It's makin' me nervous, that's what."

"That happens to a lot of people, Dottie, I mean, to a lot of people, but there's really no need to be nervous," said Gussie, trying to sound reassuring. "But you came here for more than something about cigarettes, I'll bet."

"Well, they wasn't cigarettes, that I can tell ya. They was that, whaddyacallit, mary-joo-awna stuff! So there!"

Gussie was taken aback. So far, that stuff hadn't been seen in Bickerton. This must be the first time. At least, the first *she* knew of.

"Are you sure about that, Dottie? What made you think they were marijuana? Have you seen it before?"

"No 'm, but I've smelt it an' these smelt just the same. A real stink, I calls it." She sat back in satisfaction. She'd done it. She'd reported what she'd seen. Her job was done. They could go home now. Just being in the place was getting on her nerves. She started to get up, but was stopped by Gussie.

"Hold on there just a minute," she said. "You think they *might* have been marijuana. Okay. Is there anything else you can tell me?"

"No 'm," Dottie said again, but this time it was CeeCee's turn. "Yes. There *is*. We saw her again yesterday, the minister's wife I mean. In the Cosy Corner. How she knew we were there's a mystery."

"Oh you know this town," Gussie said, "awfully hard to keep anything secret, I mean, anything secret. I'd swear sometimes the street has eyes. There's always somebody who sees what's going on, especially on Main Street. What happened then?"

"Well, she asked Dottie to give her a recipe. For the peach cobbler Dottie made for the lunch we had. And Dottie said, sure. Didn't you, Dottie?"

"For certain sure I did. Don't mind sharin'. 'Twas real simple. Ya just …"

"I'll bet it was, Dottie. And delicious too. But what happened then?"

"Well, she had this unusual pen, didn't she, Dottie?"

"Can't say as I noticed," Dottie said firmly.

"Well, she did. Couldn't help noticing at it," CeeCee said.

"Can you describe it?" Gussie asked. *Where on earth was this going?*

"Well, it was fat and silvery and had these shiny little stones all over it. Like amethysts, you know? Sort of a lavender colour? Nothing like that around here. Too fancy."

"She might have gotten it where they lived before, I mean, where they lived before," said Gussie.

"But an expensive pen like *that*? And her a *minister's* wife? Everyone knows they don't have two cents to rub together."

"Ya shoulda seen her clothes too. *An'* her shoes." Dottie didn't want to miss out.

"That isn't all," CeeCee said firmly. "I saw the writing and it was a weird purple colour. Of ink, I mean. Never seen *that* before either. Must have been awfully uncomfortable with all those fancy little stones sticking out. Writing with it, I mean."

Gussie's heart lurched. Trying not to appear too eager, she said, "Did you notice the colour of paper she was writing on?"

"Sure did," CeeCee replied. "Couldn't miss it. Took them both out of her purse at the same time. Pen *and* paper. That cheap yellow stuff. Not a nice paper at all. For a fancy pen like that, you'd think …"

Gussie was scribbling like mad on her own pad of paper which was a snowy white. She couldn't stand the colour yellow. She looked up. "Well, it's getting close on dinner time. No need to keep you here any longer. Thank you both for coming in. I'll be looking into this first thing tomorrow, I mean, first thing. Don't worry now. Everything you've told me today will be kept inside this office. You can be sure of that." As they got up to leave, she added, "You two would make great detectives." Before they said goodbye, she said, "And can I ask you to keep it to yourselves, what you've told me? For now, I mean? You will? And thanks again."

After the two women left, Gussie sat back in her chair. She was the one who was stunned now. *The minister's wife? She's the individual who's been writing those letters? Her? But why? What possible reason could she have for doing such a thing?*

31
COLD FEET?

After thinking about what had been found at the old farm, and worse, what might be still waiting to be discovered, Rab was having second thoughts. Not only would the police be hanging around up there for a while, Dottie's reaction to even the slightest possibility something terrible must have happened there would spoil his pleasure at having found a place he could afford. And the chance to grow his own vegetables. Maybe he'd been expecting too much of his sister who was such a willing worker. And CeeCee too, of course. But then, if she went and married that Gene fella, she'd be lost to them, wouldn't she? He'd figured the two women could run the store while he was up supervising the farm. He'd have to hire someone to live there all the time. But then, he'd known that from the beginning. It was too far away to be left sitting on its own. No doubt there'd be a ton of wild animals – rabbits and coons and such – that would just love the taste of any kind of vegetable. And then there was the added problem of getting the stuff back down to East Tee.

He broached the subject to Dottie one evening after the supper dishes were done and CeeCee was out with Gene again. Jesse had gone to bed early, said he was plumb tuckered out from all the shelving he'd done that day. He was hoping to hear from his pop the next day about visiting his mom over in Dunhampton General.

"What's the matter? Gettin' cold feet, are ya?" was Dottie's terse response. "Ya brought it on yourself, Dougal Kibbidge, ya never ast me a thing, just pushed ahead an' bought the place. I coulda tole ya ta think on it a mite longer, but no, ya hadda rush into it."

Dougal? She must really be sore at me. She only calls me that when she's really ticked off. Aloud he said, "Sorry, Dot, didn't ever imagine there'd be anythin' wrong with the place. 'Specially somethin' like this. You're dead right. I shoulda talked it over with you. But it was such a good buy an' I thought …"

"That's the trouble in a nutshell. Ya didn't think. Ya work so hard for your money, ya should take more care to see where it goes at."

"Well, I guess I gotta see this thing through now. Us Kibbidges don't give up that easy. Do you think we could close the store Mondays? Most everyone else does. Out here, anyways. Stay closed for two days in a row, I mean."

"Now, don't go changin' how we does things that quick. Me an' CeeCee kin manage fine. Could be young Jess'll be here longer than we think. His pop called an' ast me if we could keep him here after school starts. That is, if Kitty hasta stay over to Dunhampton till goin' on October."

"He won't like that too much," said Rab, "havin' to go to school over here."

"Needs must when the devil drives, ya know that as well as me, Rab," Dottie replied.

Rab! Guess I'm back in her good books again. Better smarten up 'n let her know what I'm up to the next time. If there is one.

32
THE MYSTERY DEEPENS

Gussie knew there was nothing for it but to ask Dr. Bill Blair to go up to the old farm with her. She hated the idea of being in the same car with the guy. He was so darned persistent in trying to get her to go out with him. But he was the Acting Coroner, had been for ages. He had to be taken to the scene of any suspicious death. No two ways about it. Why couldn't she make him see she had no intention of ever getting involved with him? She suddenly had an idea. If Syd came up with her in his truck, she'd tell the doc he'd have to come in his own car. By rights, he should have come the first time, but she hadn't really believed Rab's bone story. She'd had to see it for herself.

Now she was feeling faint stirrings of doubt that it *was* a settler's grave. Too shallow. In fact, it was more like a depression. A slight dip in the land. She also knew she shouldn't have collected the bones on her own. The doc should have seen them before they'd been moved. Too late now. But no one had to know she'd bent the rules again. At least she hoped not. Her impulses had gotten the better of her again. Like the time she took young Jesse Woodcock into the woods to look for a body he said he'd seen. And anyway, she'd left lots of tiny fragments of bone behind and only taken the larger ones.

Those two auxiliaries seemed like good guys to her. They'd keep their mouths shut. And so would Syd. She doubted anyone in the Kibbidge household would breathe a word. So she'd have to pretend to the doc this boneyard thing was news to her. And she wasn't going to tell him what she suspected might be at the bottom of the well. Or, the biggest secret of all, that only she knew: while Rusty and Mike were busy hauling the rocks out of the well, she'd ventured further, over into the dense woods. Well beyond where the boneyard lay. And had stumbled across something else.

Later on, when she'd had time to think about it, she didn't know why she'd done it. She thought it must have been a gut feeling that led her there. After she'd pushed her way into the undergrowth a little way, she spotted something odd. It looked like an old shed, partially collapsed in on itself and barely visible. *What in heck? Why here? Miles away from the other buildings?* Her curiosity really aroused now, she squeezed past a group of young ash trees blocking the way and swept aside the curtains of the wild cucumber vines that dangled everywhere.

A frayed piece of what looked like tarpaulin hung suspended over what was left of the opening into the shed. When she'd gotten past it, and avoided some rotten boards bristling with nails, she could see the shape of a vehicle surrounded by piles of dead leaves and weeds. A little closer and the vehicle turned out to be an old Willys Jeep, a relic from the War years. Covered with cobwebs.

Brushing the cobwebs away so she could peer through the dingy window, she could just barely make out a heap of something grayish white on the front seat. When she tried the door, she was surprised that it opened easily enough. Odd. It creaked like the opening door at the beginning of that old radio show, *The Inner Sanctum*. But it did open. Oh no! Not more bones! But these weren't human bones. Far too small. Maybe they were animal bones. She reached around behind her. Luckily she still had a spare bag in her back pocket. Scooping as many bones as she could into the bag, she closed the door. *I'll have to come back in here with a flashlight. Too dark to inspect it properly under all these trees and vines. But gee whiz! What's it doing away up here anyway?*

Later that day, after she'd taken care of what's known in police jargon as a domestic, and gotten the couple involved calmed down, making them promise to go for counselling or she'd be back, she managed to reach Syd. He'd been out chasing down a story about someone trying to set up a snake farm near East Tee.

"Can't talk long. Got a deadline to meet, you know. There's this guy wants to raise pythons and boa constrictors, if you can believe it. He thinks people should be educated about snakes. Out here, of all places. He probably couldn't get a licence to do it in the City."

"This is the first I've heard about it," Gussie said, disgustedly. "As far as I know, he hasn't applied for any kind of licence. I don't think he's going to get what he wants here either. Oh boy, that's all I need, I mean, that's all I need. Dangerous snakes getting loose and terrorizing … no! It isn't going to happen."

"Well, I'm going to write it up anyway. How do you like this for a headline? **SNAKE SLITHERS INTO SCHOOL, STARTLES STUDENTS.** Sorry. I couldn't resist that." He could hear Gussie snorting on the other end of the line. "Uh, what were you calling for?"

After she could get control of herself, Gussie explained. When Syd asked when she wanted to go, she told him, "ASAP. I mean, as soon as I can get a hold of the doc. Hopefully day after tomorrow. The weather's supposed to be pretty good for the next few days, I mean, the next few days."

"Yeah. You bet. I'm keen. But, uh, Gus, you sure it's okay this time? Let me know when you set it up. Mmm bye bye, for nc *N*." And he was gone.

Snakes! What next? Maybe a whole zoo? Not while I'm on the job. So now I better call the doc and tell him about the old farm. Good thing Syd'll come. Be good protection against Loverboy Blair!

33
A NEW CRIME IN TOWN?

The starchy nurse - at least that's how Gussie always thought of her, being as overprotective of the doctor as she was – Dr. Blair's nurse, who invariably answered the phone at his office, said he was unavailable. When Gussie tried to tell her it was important work for the coroner, she insisted, even more abruptly, he was *unavailable*. To *anyone*. And no, she couldn't say why. Or wouldn't, was more than likely the case. She did say he was expected back in a couple of days. And what's more, she didn't take messages unless the caller was really ill and needed professional advice. Meaning from her. And she hung up.

Plopping the phone back on its cradle, Gussie thought maybe she should have gone over to the clinic in person. But no. If there happened to be patients in the waiting room, they'd be upset when she showed up. In uniform. They'd be thinking one of them must be in trouble, for sure. They only ever saw Constable Gussie in uniform when there was trouble. Or a street fair. Or a parade. So she'd have to take nursie's word for it.

It was going to be another 'hot, hazy, and humid' day, according to the weather report on the local radio station COBB. Most of the time they get it right, but the Great Lakes area is notorious for changeable weather. Hard to predict, as one of the weather guys told Gussie at some meeting or other. Not the greatest weather for working. But maybe a good day to look into the story of the strange cigarettes and the minister's wife.

Gussie decided to take the bull by the horns and go over to the parsonage and nose around. It came to her she had the perfect excuse: she could use her revived relationship with Syd to find out what was involved in going through a second marriage ceremony. There was no way they were going to live together without it. She needed all the credibility she could get in this town. So did Syd, for that matter. And cohabitation was frowned on. Shacking up, they called it. How crude that sounded.

The Rev. Simon Essery was home, all right, but was not at all happy at being interrupted. This was the day he worked on his sermon, and although the one for the next service was being revamped from one he'd given at the last church, it needed some changes. He was now in a small town, not a much larger one like the previous town. And many of his congregants were rural folk, so it had to be redirected at them. So to speak. Any interruption and he'd have to start all over again.

Pink and grey fieldstones had been used in the construction of the century-old parsonage known as 'The Rockpile', conveniently located directly across the street from the church. Gussie tried knocking several times on the solid oak front door. Getting no response, even though she could see a car parked in the garage, she went around to the side door and leaned on the bell until a grumpy unshaven reverend finally opened it. She was surprised to find him alone. As she told Syd later, in her experience, ministers' wives didn't used to gad about so much. Or even have their own cars. Always bustling around, busy in the soup kitchen, or meeting with some church group, or organizing a fundraiser for the church, or even practising the piano. They weren't supposed to have lives of their own. Maybe things had changed when she hadn't been looking.

"Why he told me his wife wasn't home, I don't know. I hadn't even asked for her. I guess he just assumed I was there to see her, not him. That struck me as odd right off the bat, I mean, right off the bat," Gussie said. "Don't people usually call on the clergyman if they want something? And not his wife?"

"Yeah, they do," Syd said. "So what happened next? Come on, Gus, speed it up. I've got ..."

"Oh well, if you're too busy to listen, we can leave the rest for ..."

"No way, you're not going to leave me in suspenders. Not this time. What happened then?"

Somewhat mollified, Gussie continued. "As soon as I got in the door, I started sneezing. Some kind of strong smell was in the air. Smelled to me like camphor. You know? That stuff that's supposed to keep the moths away? That made me even more suspicious, I mean, even more suspicious. It just didn't smell right to me."

"Do you think he might have been trying to hide the smell of something else? Like fried onions? Or fish?"

"Nope, nothing like that. Just wait till I tell you. I mentioned the possibility of us getting married again."

"Oh Gus, did you mean it? You weren't just …"

"Didn't we decide that the other night? After the lights went out? Or did I just imagine it after all that wine? Anyway, it was a good excuse to get him talking," Gussie said. "When I told him what we were planning to do, he said we'd have to come and see him together to discuss it. I said I'd tell you. And then I asked him if he'd heard about anyone using marijuana here in town, I mean, here in town. He turned several shades of green when I said that. He asked me why I wanted to know. So I came right out with it and said someone had reported seeing some. I didn't say where, but he started coughing. He coughed so hard he practically choked, I mean, he practically choked! He disappeared into the kitchen and I heard the water running. When he came back, he asked me to sit down. I knew I had him then. And then he started talking about his troubles with his stepson. From his wife's first marriage. He said it wasn't known in town that she even had a son. Or that she'd been married before, I mean, married before. Not yet anyway."

"Hmm. Wonder how that tidbit escaped the local gossip mill? Go on. Then what?"

"Well, he hemmed and he hawed and then he finally said this stepson was constantly in trouble. With the law. He wasn't just exactly sure why, but when he caught his wife smoking something illegal – he wouldn't say the name out loud – he had to ask her where she got it and she said from Travis. Said she'd just wanted to see what it was like. And then it wasn't too long before she found herself hooked on the stuff, I mean, hooked on the stuff. The next thing he knew, she was, well, she was, and then he nearly broke down. You know how everyone dumps their problems on the minister? Well, I wonder who does he dump his on?" She paused for breath and to listen if anyone had come in to the front office. She'd told Myrna to hold her calls but forgot to mention visitors.

"Oh. My. God. You mean she was *dealing*? And no one knew? Is that possible?" Syd was mystified. He hadn't heard anything about the dreaded weed showing up in Bickerton. It must be the fault of the hippy types who came out on weekends from the City. Maybe this Travis character was one of them. What a story this would make! But he had to hear the rest before he decided whether or not to make an issue of it.

"Go on, Gus. What did he say then?"

"He said it was the reason they'd left the last three places. He was afraid his wife would get caught and then he'd be out of a job, I mean, out of a job. And a reputation."

"That's for sure. No church wants someone like that telling them to be honest. And straight. And good. Or telling them how to live. In any way, shape, or form. Daffy did say the Church Council hadn't checked out his story before they hired him, they were so anxious to grab him before anyone else did because they thought he was such a good preacher. If this gets out, well …"

"Yeah, that *would* be a scandal. The church is having a hard enough time as it is. Keeping their people, I mean. Anyway, he practically got down on his knees and begged me to give him another chance to get her to stop. He was half crying when he said that, I mean, half crying. He said she'd promised to quit before they came here and he thought she had. Until yesterday, when he found a couple of butts floating in the toilet, I mean, floating in the toilet. With lipstick on them. Dear Travis had been there the day before. Just out on parole. Figures."

Syd wasn't satisfied. Not yet. Gussie had already told him about the visit from CeeCee and Dottie and what they'd seen. So in true newsman's fashion, he had to ask, "Did you get to the poison pen stuff? Daffy told me the other day there haven't been any more of them. Letters, I mean. Or phone calls, for that matter. Not for the past week or so."

"No I didn't. I want to talk to Mrs. Essery herself. Confront her, I mean. But she was away. Gone shopping in the City, her husband said. He hadn't a clue when she'd be back. Might be a couple of days for all he knew. He looked really miserable, I mean, really miserable when he said that. I guess she spends a lot of time off on her own." Gussie thought for a minute. "You know, this might be the reason why he's so nervous around the people in the church. And acts so weird with Daffy, I mean, with Daffy. With her especially, as she's right there in the church office. He's all alone dealing with this thing. And he's scared stiff." She sighed. "I have to say I'm almost sorry for the poor guy."

"Poor guy, nothing. If there's crooked stuff going on, a minister and his wife are no better than anyone else."

"Don't I know it," Gussie said, ruefully. "But still, what has to be done is up to me. Isn't it?"

34
DING DONG BELL ...

... *pussy's in the well ... who put her in ... little Johnny Flynn ...* The words to the old nursery rhyme kept running through Gussie's head as she and Syd made their way up to the old farm. Full of anticipation, she could hardly wait to see if her suspicions about what they might find in the well would turn out to be the right ones. She'd had a call from the auxiliaries who'd gone back up a couple of days before and managed to remove the sewer cover and the gridwork of heavy iron bars they'd discovered under the rocks when they'd been there the last time. Why would someone have gone to all the trouble of cementing in iron bars to keep the rocks from falling into the water below? If they didn't have something unspeakable to hide?

Behind them, trying hard not to show his intense annoyance, came the small sports car of Dr. Blair. The brand new two-seater was a bright orange you could see a mile away. The young doctor was more than dismayed to find Gussie's ex-husband took precedence over him. In fact, he was downright furious. After all, *he* was the coroner. And this would have been a first-class chance to persuade the reluctant lady cop to go out with him. He was sure, given time, she'd come around.

Her ex seemed like a nice enough guy, though. Maybe that was the problem. He was too nice. What Gussie needed was a guy with more experience of the world. And more money to spend on her. Not a guy who ran a rinky-dink weekly paper in a rinky-dink kind of a town. The only reason he'd taken over the medical practice in Bickerton, after a couple of years in the Far North, was to gain enough experience to tackle the Big City. He had his eye on a practice he'd heard would become available in another year or so. It was in the heart of Downtown Toronto close to the largest hospital. When he left, he'd take Gussie with him after convincing her to give up this nonsense of chasing petty crooks out here in the boonies and exposing herself to all kinds of danger. He didn't know it yet, but he was doomed to be disappointed.

The day had started out fair enough, but now sullen gray clouds were slowly rolling in from the southwest. Gradually the sun was being swallowed up. At first, Gussie thought the low-lying clouds looked like smoke. She hoped the woods weren't on fire somewhere. This was the time of year for late night bush parties when campfires sometimes got out of control. Nothing special had come through on the police radio other than a report of another major traffic delay on the main highway. A bus had collided with a transport truck west of Dunhampton. But no report of any forest fires.

A light wind had come up and the leaves of the trees along the road were starting to lift and show their undersides. A sure sign of a storm coming, Mac used to say. Gussie hoped and prayed it would hold off long enough for the coroner to inspect the place and for her to take another look at the hidden shed. With Syd of course. She was determined not to be in a position where she was alone with the doctor.

When the pleasure of being together had settled into a companionable silence, Syd, who could never stay quiet for long, brought up the subject of Slackerville and what might have happened there.

"Hey, Gus, I haven't had a chance to tell you, but the other night when I couldn't sleep, I remembered this funny old guy who came in to the *Bugler* to see Dad a couple of times. Years ago. He was a bit of a recluse. If he remembers Dad, he might remember something. If he's still alive, that is. I think he was living in the bush somewhere north of here. He used to come into town for supplies every once in a while. Sometimes he and Dad would go over to the Cosy Corner and Dad would stand him to a meal. I checked in the *Bugler's* morgue to see if this guy had ever been interviewed. A total waste of time. I couldn't think of his name. Must have been unusual. Foreign or something. I guess I didn't pay much attention to the stories Dad was working on back then. Typical of young people though, isn't it? Too busy with their own lives. Too self-centred, I guess you could say."

Gussie glanced up at what she could see of the sky through the dusty windshield. Still more clouds coming. And they were clouds all right, not smoke. She was beginning to think they might have to turn around and give it up for today.

Without waiting for her to respond, Syd went on. "Next thing I hunted up was the old telephone books. We got stacks of 'em buried way back in the morgue. I thought if I saw the name I might recognize it. But then I realized it isn't likely he'd have had a phone. Not in the back of beyond. Tomorrow I'll go to the Town Hall and look through the old records." He put a tentative hand on her knee. "Hey, this detective work sure isn't all that easy, is it? Anyway, what say I nose around and try to find out if the old geezer is still alive? And where he lives now? There's just got to be somebody still around who remembers the story." He glanced over at Gussie and was fascinated by her intensity as they bucketed along. *Wonder what she's thinking now? I'd almost forgotten how she is when she gets her teeth into a job. When she's on a case, she's like a cat after a mouse. Poor mouse doesn't stand a chance!*

Her eyes fixed firmly on the road ahead, Gussie was trying to keep her speed constant. She didn't want the doc getting too close to her. The wind was picking up now and buffeted the truck whenever they passed an opening in the woods. It was getting harder to stay on the road. She hoped they weren't in for the kind of blow they'd suffered through a couple of years ago when over half of Bickerton's big trees were uprooted and many roofs lost their shingles. Luckily, that storm had come through very early in the morning when no one was up and about. When full daylight finally came, everyone was shocked to see one of the churches was missing its steeple. It had been sheared right off. Somehow the unsettled feeling in the air was starting to remind her of that terrible time.

Syd tried again. "Hey, Gus, do you think maybe you shouldn't spend so much time on this, uh, cold case, don't they call it now? After all, there could be ..."

This last was too much for Gussie, who gave him a sharp sideways look. "Syd Spilsbury! You know perfectly well there's no such thing! There's only the ones no one's figured out yet, I mean, figured out. Besides, this one's important. Mr. Kibbidge's got himself a piece of property where obviously something happened and it's up to me, or up to us I should say, to find out what it was. And now that I know about it, I simply have to follow through, don't I? Anyway, you're forgetting how much help he was with the Denton thing, I mean, with the Denton thing."

"Don't they call him Rab?" said Syd, quickly changing the subject. "What kind of a name is Rab anyway? I hear he doesn't like to be called Mr. Kibbidge."

Gussie shifted in her seat. They were getting close to the turn-off for the old farm and she, for one, would be happy to see it. There was a sameness to the countryside up this way. Evergreens by the hundreds, probably done in a fit of reforestation by the government. Planted over twenty-five years ago. Maple, ash and oak - all wedged so tightly together you couldn't see into them. Brush of all kinds crowding the edges of the road. With every once in a while a glimpse of abandoned pastureland.

"It's short for rabbit," she said tartly. "Dottie told me he used to raise them when he was a kid. Rabbits, I mean. Everyone got to calling him the Rabbit Man and after a while the Rab part stuck. I think his real name's Dougal. And what you said before? Good idea about the old guy. Go ahead and see what you can turn up, I mean, what you can turn up." She took a deep breath. "Can we please not talk for a few minutes? I've got to make sure I don't miss the sideroad. Not marked for some reason, I mean, for some reason." She glanced again in the rear view mirror. The doc's orange car clung close behind. Almost like a trailer. *Hey, the crazy guy's tailgating us! Hope he has the sense to slow down some. That's a powerful little machine.*

Syd peered at the side mirror. It was chipped and cracked, but you could still see what was behind. *Gee, that guy's kinda close. Better not say anything to Gus. Sure she's already noticed.*

In the two-seater, Bill Blair was fuming. Through the small window in the back of the truck's cab he could see them talking. And sitting close together. And he didn't like it. *Am I jealous? You're darn tooting I am! That should be me up there with her. Not him. He had his chance with her and he blew it. What does she see in the guy anyway? And look at his old beater of a truck! What a joke! I bet once I take her for a spin in this peppy little set of wheels, she'll soon see what she's missing.*

He suddenly realized Gussie was braking and signalling a turn. The dark blue truck abruptly veered to the right. But the brakes on the little orange car were quick and Blair sailed around the corner without incident. *Where in heck are we? Looks like the ends of the earth. This is The Wilderness for sure!*

35
PLAYING THE WAITING GAME

Lying flat on an unforgiving hospital bed in her lonely room close to the small maternity section of Dunhampton General, Kitty had to admit it. She was bored. If she had to be stuck in here for weeks on end, she'd have much preferred to be in the ward down the hall than stuck in a private room. At least, there'd be some life there. Sometimes she could hear their voices. And sometimes laughter. It made her feel lonelier than ever. But Albie insisted she be by herself. Dr. Blair told him - more than once - his wife must have absolute peace and quiet. Nothing that might overstimulate her, like conversation. Otherwise, she might lose the babies.

Dottie and CeeCee had visited her twice and Albie brought Jesse to see her a couple of times. But they never stayed very long. Jesse looked so miserable when he had to leave that Kitty was forced to hold back her tears until he and Albie were out of sight. She didn't want to upset Jess any more than she could help. Poor kid, having to stay all week with the Kibbidges when Albie was away. Not that she was ungrateful for their concern. Not at all. For people who'd never had children of their own, they were doing a real good job. But then she realized she was forgetting CeeCee still lived there and had had two children. But girls, not boys. Boys were different somehow. Jesse was always properly dressed and certainly looked like he was getting enough to eat. He said Mister Rab never gave him a job that was too much for him. But she knew he was missing home. And her too, of course. Good thing he had the pup to keep him company. Especially at night.

She tried to turn on her side, but the shifting weight of the babies made it too uncomfortable. Every move she made caused the plastic under the bottom sheet to crackle. What a nuisance. The coarse hospital sheets made her poor skin sore and even raw in some places. She hated to complain, the nurses were so nice. It wasn't their fault the bed linen was so cheap. She guessed it had to be tough enough to stand up to hot water and bleach.

Last time Dottie and CeeCee had been in to see her, they told her about the old neglected farm. Rab wanted a place to grow his own vegetables, they said. They thought it was too far from East Tee, but he got a real deal, they said. For back taxes and a bit more, they said. Kitty didn't tell them she already knew about it from Jesse, but wanted to hear what they had to say. They'd hinted that something strange had happened up there. Years ago they thought, and Constable Gussie was investigating. That was all.

When Jesse came the next day, she found she didn't want to get into it with him. Not while she was here in the hospital. But she couldn't help but wonder what the strange event could have been. In the backwoods, of all places. And just *how* strange? She tried to restrain her imagination on that one and hoped Jess didn't know anything about it. There were days when it was obvious to her he was remembering the body in the woods.

Focussing on the huge bouquet of flowers he'd brought, she tried not to worry about him. He'd always seemed like such a sensitive kid. But he could be tough in his own way. He'd taken the news of twins in his stride. She'd been afraid he might be upset with two babies coming at once. But all he said was he hoped one was a boy. He said he didn't know much about girls. *Not yet, he doesn't and thank goodness for that,* was all his mother could think. *Time enough for that. Hope I'm up to handling it. When it happens.*

36
FACE OFF

The grit-filled dust swirled around the truck as they pulled into the old farm. Along the lane, the two lonely poplar trees were being whipped back and forth by the wind. As they passed, the top of one of them snapped off and was quickly carried away. Gussie and Syd climbed out of the truck and zipped up their windbreakers. Syd patted his pocket to make sure he had his notebook with him, while Gussie collected the hard hats from the back of the truck. She handed one to Syd who plopped it on his head.

"Gonna need these," she said while putting on her own. "I don't want any of us to get hit on the head with something, the wind's so strong. Be sure to do up the strap good and tight."

"This is as far as we can go!" she shouted back to the doctor who had just gotten out of his car. "Gotta hoof it the rest of the way!" The doctor stared at his car ruefully, hoping the finish wouldn't get too dirty or scratched even. He always wanted his cars to look as though they'd just been driven out of the showroom. Maybe he should have kept his old car for times like this. He never thought he'd have to go this far into the bush, being blissfully ignorant of what it could be like in Southern Ontario. He'd thought it was all farmland and mostly open space. Hah!

The wind seemed to slacken off a little as they made their way around the old house and up to the area where the boneyard was. The doctor stopped at the sight of the sweep of blue stretching up behind the house. *Looks like those weeds they say are supposed to bring bad luck. From the sound of it, whoever lived here sure had a good dose of that.*

As they approached the well site, Gussie went on ahead to see what it looked like with the iron grid out of the way.

"Would you look at this!" she said as the others caught up with her. The doctor was already out of breath. Funny. He'd thought he was in pretty good shape. Trying not to let the other two see his distress, he reached up to adjust his hard hat. Syd took one look into the well and stepped back.

"Don't think we'll see too much here," he said. "Water's way up. Guess you'll have to get the thing drained or something before you can see all the way to the bottom."

"Hold on a sec, will you?" And Gussie took a square black flashlight out of her pocket. "This thing's guaranteed to penetrate even the darkest night. Let's see what it can do with deep water." She moved closer to the well and, switching it on, aimed the light into the depths. At first the water was too disturbed by the wind to be able to see properly. The minute it settled, she realized it was a shimmering opalescent green. She swung around and handed the flashlight to the doctor. "Here, Doc. Take a look."

The doctor, who was still trying to get his bearings and not being exactly sure what was going on, shone the light into the well. Once his eyes had gotten used to the gloom, he gasped and said, "What the heck?"

It was Syd's turn to try out the light. "Holy smoke! Looks like a pile of bones down there! In fact, looks to me like part of a skeleton. Or maybe more than one!"

"That's what I thought," Gussie said. "And you, Doc, what do you see?"

"Same here," responded the doctor. "Like Syd said, you'll have to get rid of the water."

"Well, it won't be today, anyway. That sky isn't showing any signs of clearing up and I think it might rain. I hope we have time to check out the boneyard before it does."

The doctor found himself losing patience. *More walking. And up another hill! And this one's even steeper. Wow, those two sure are quick! Hope my old ticker can stand the pace.* He'd certainly never banked on the coroner's job being this much work. Since he'd come to Bickerton, he could count on the fingers of one hand the number of times he'd had to view bodies. And so far, that had been in the small makeshift morgue at the back of his office. Not anything nearly as strenuous as this.

They finally reached the boneyard where Gussie had left some large tree branches over the spot where she'd found the bones. As she and Syd started to drag them aside, they were startled to see the doctor come up behind them and abruptly sit down on a nearby stump. He was almost totally done in. This time he made no effort to hide his breathlessness.

Gussie dropped the branch she'd been shifting and came over to take a look. "Boy, you'd better just stay put for minute. You don't look so good, I mean, so good," was her only comment. *Physician, heal thyself,* Syd was thinking, trying hard not to feel sorry for the guy. But he did look kind of pathetic sitting there all hunched up. A couple of times he put his head down between his knees. Syd remembered Gussie telling him her dad said that was a good thing to do if you were feeling faint. He hoped the doctor wasn't having an attack of some kind. What in blue blazes could they do with him away out here in the back of beyond?

After few minutes, the doctor stood up.

"Not to worry," he said. "My heart does this sometimes. I had rheumatic fever as a child and it weakened my heart somehow."

The other two looked at each other in relief. They told him he should take it easy. They'd clear off the branches. It wouldn't take long. As soon as they were finished, the doctor moved over to the depression where Gussie said there were bones. After squatting down and taking a closer look, he said he couldn't understand why there were only a few scattered fragments. He turned to Gussie.

"I thought you said it might be a gravesite. Nothing here to indicate that," he said crossly.

Gussie looked a bit sheepish. "Well, I took some of them home. Bones, I mean."

"Why on earth did you do that? You know the rules. You *know* you should have waited until I saw them first. What did you do with them?"

"I packed them off to the lab in the City. I should be getting the results any day now, I mean, any day now. Then we'll know whether it was a man or a woman or …"

But that wasn't good enough for the doctor. He said again she should have waited for him to examine the place properly. She could be in serious trouble, he went on. Syd told him to simmer down and stay put. He said he and Gussie had one more place they had to check and pointed up the hill. At that, the doctor lost his temper.

"Hold on a minute there! *I* should be the one going up there with Gussie! Not *you*, Syd. This is *my* business, not yours! You're only a small town newsman, not a doctor. You probably didn't even finish high school."

All his jealousy, seeing the two of them so close together, shutting him out, all his dismay that his miserable heart had let him down again, all his frustration over losing another chance with Gussie, began to boil over. His face flushing a deep scarlet, he took a step closer to Syd and clenched his fists.

Realizing the situation was turning ugly, Gussie quickly stepped between them.

"This is no way for a professional to act," she said sharply. "And you *are* a professional, are you not? I know you're mad because I won't go out with you. But you'd better know this. Syd and I are getting married again, I mean, getting married again. Next month, in fact. And I asked him to come with us today because it's *his* job to let the people in Bickerton know what we find here, I mean, what we find here. And until we can figure out just exactly what might have happened here, he won't say a word to anyone!"

Syd put a restraining hand on her arm. "Aw, come on, doc," he said. "We were just trying to save you the trouble of climbing away up there into the woods to look at something Gussie found. We saw how hard it's been for you to get this far. We don't want anything to happen to you. We sure as heck wouldn't know what to do if it did." And although the doctor had insulted him, he tried to say this as calmly as he could. *Wouldn't want the doctor to think I'm patronizing him. Holy cow! The guy's gone red as a beet! Must be something wrong with him for sure. And he isn't that much older than I am!*

37
EMPTY COOP

If anyone had chanced to come by the office at Saint Peeps Church that day, they would have seen an unusual sight: the normally shy church secretary with her arms around the minister, trying her best to comfort him. He was blubbering like a baby, his head on her shoulder.

At first, Daffy had been alarmed. On her way to work that morning, she'd decided it was about time she caught up on the filing. The heavy four-drawer cabinet had never been moved into the outer office space she occupied, so it was still in the main office where the previous minister wanted it. When she went to take the Rev. Simon Essery's mail in to him, she was startled to see the reverend lying across his desk, supporting his head on his arms. And on a Wednesday! He'd never come in on a Wednesday before. She stopped in the doorway for a minute to listen. He was mumbling words she recognized from the 23rd Psalm. ... *walk ... through ... the valley ... of ... the shadow ... of death ...* Dropping the mail on a chair, she quickly moved over to him. Soft hearted soul that she was, she couldn't bear to see him like that, even though she was still a little afraid of him.

When she asked him in soothing tones what was wrong, he shook his head and what she could see of his face crumpled. She decided a drink of something might help - why she didn't know - but it was all she could think of. It would take too long to make tea, so after assuring him she'd be right back, she hurried to the church kitchen to run him a glass of water. Trying not to spill it, she went back to his office as fast as she could. When she got there, she found him sitting up, staring at nothing. He seized the glass and downed it in one go. Setting the glass firmly on the desk, he turned to her and said huskily, "I never thought to see this day. Never, never, *never!*" And then he burst into tears.

Even while Daffy was telling Gussie about it, she still found it hard to believe. After he'd calmed down some and blown his nose into an enormous handkerchief, the reverend said his wife had disappeared two days before. Without saying a word to him or even leaving him a note. He choked up when he said that and blew his nose again. She'd taken her passport and some money and was gone. He'd been out visiting a sick member of his flock and when he got home, the house was dark and silent. He knew right away from the state of their bedroom that she'd packed up in a hurry.

Daffy could hardly get the words out fast enough. Gussie had to tell her to slow down. The secretary took a couple of deep breaths and continued. The reverend said he shouldn't have told his wife about Constable Spilsbury's visit. He said he guessed it must have spooked her somehow and she'd gone off to some relative or other down in South Carolina. Or was it North Carolina? He couldn't remember which. In any case, he'd never met the so-called relative. If that's who it was. Her son Travis had phoned him early the next morning to tell him where she'd gone and not to bother trying to find her. At least the poor reverend knew that much.

"Gussie, I swear these were his exact words! 'She flew the coop on me, Bertie did. She flew the coop! And all this time I thought she *loved* me. I know I love *her*. Terribly. We could have worked this out together. But this way - this way she's turned herself into a fugitive. And I can't help her!'"

Daffy leaned forward and continued, "I thought he might start bawling again at any moment. Honestly, Gussie, I had *no idea* of what he might do next. I was half afraid he might go home and do something terrible to himself. And I didn't even know there *was* a son! Or should I say stepson. At least, that's what the reverend called him. Did you?" She clasped her hands together and unclasped them again.

Gussie held her tongue. Daffy didn't need to know the details of her visit to the pastor.

"What happened then?" Gussie asked, to show she was paying attention. *This story is getting crazier by the minute!*

"He said after he got the phone call, he came straight over to the church. At first, he tried to pray in the sanctuary, but the words refused to come. So he retreated to his office where he thought no one could hear him. Then he broke down. That's when I showed up. And when he told me he knew his wife was the one who'd sent those letters and made those phone calls, well … I've never been so shocked in all my life! The minister's wife! Of all people! But why would she go and do something like that? Why? *Why?*"

Throughout this lengthy revelation, Gussie was trying hard not to show her surprise.

"Could be she was hoping the Board would kick him out if they thought he had a shady past, I mean, a shady past. And then he could look for a job somewhere else that paid better," was her quick response. *Gee, I didn't think that one through very carefully, did I? But it's odd how it's always the ones you least suspect. What on earth should I be doing now about this nasty business? At least the identity of the poison pen's no longer a mystery. Maybe the whole sorry mess is out of my hands. Or is it?*

38
QUESTIONS, QUESTIONS

When they finally got back down to Bickerton after the awful day up at the old farm, Gussie told Syd she was sorry but she was just too tired to talk about it and she'd call him after she'd had a chance to sort things out. Say, in a day or two. And not to say a word to anyone like he'd promised.

"Aw, Gus, you of all people know I'm man of my word. There won't be a drop of ink spent on this story or even a whisper from me till you say so," he said, giving her a lingering hug and kiss. He sure hoped he could sit on this story. For a couple more days anyway. But it wouldn't be easy. He was relieved the doctor wouldn't be pestering her any more. At least, he hoped the guy got the message. The thought of being back with Gussie again made his heart soar. There'd never been anyone else for him. Never would be either. Now, to get rid of the *Bugler*.

Back at her apartment, Gussie opened a can of tomato soup, stirred in some milk and made toast while the soup was warming up. That was all she felt like eating. She hunted up the remains of a bottle of wine and filled a tumbler with what was left.

Sitting at her kitchen table, her head in a whirl, she took a couple of sips of wine and started in on the soup. Try as she might, she couldn't figure out what could possibly have happened up at the old farm. Syd said he was still trying to find the name of the old guy who used to live up around there. Maybe he could help them out. If he was still alive. It was a long shot. But anything she could find out would be a help.

In between bites of toast, she scribbled down a list of questions that would have to have answers. *Were the bones in the well from the people who'd lived in the old house? How many people were there? We could see at least two skulls. Are there more? How long had the bones been in the well? What did the bones up the hill have to do with it? And why were there bones in the old Jeep? And – why was the Jeep away up there in the first place?*

With a sigh, she dropped her pencil and decided she was too tired to concentrate on anything more. After a good hot shower, she went straight to bed and tried to sleep. But tired as she was, she couldn't get the memory of the day out of her head. The doctor, poor soul, admitting he had a physical weakness which had surprised both her and Syd. And then him coming close to punching Syd out. Well, that was too much. Too much altogether. She should have been firmer with the guy when he tried to get a date with her.

On the way back down to their vehicles, Dr. Blair was still fuming. Kicking angrily at the Blue Devils as they passed through them, he'd threatened again to report her 'theft' of the bones to her bosses over in Dunhampton. Said he could make things tough for her. She'd had to think fast on that one. As quickly as she could, she retorted that if he did, she could make it equally tough on him. When he laughed and told her not to be ridiculous, she'd said, 'Then where were *you* for the last little while, going off and leaving your practice in the hands of that stuffy old nurse? You weren't around when I wanted you to come up to the farm. Did you forget you're supposed to let me know when you go out of town?' He'd shut up after that. And all the while the gusts of wind were swirling around them in fits and starts. Flattening Blue Devils to the ground. Blowing dirt in their faces. And then it started spitting rain. It had been like a scene in a B movie. She finally drifted off, dreaming about Syd. A sweet dream after all the turmoil of the day.

39
SHAKE-UP AT SAINT PEEPS

The Sunday after Bertie Essery disappeared, the congregation of Saint Peeps was shocked to arrive at the church at the usual time and discover they had no minister. The choir leader was standing inside the front door where the minister usually stood to welcome people as they came in. Dix said only good morning all, welcome, and please take your places. Then he moved up to the organ and played a short Bach prelude. When the time came for the service to start, the choir filed in to *'Holy, holy, holy'*, that well known hymn that has been sung forever to get things rolling. After the last notes died away, Dix went over to the lectern and spoke into the microphone.

"Welcome, everyone, to Sts. Peter and Paul Union Church. Isn't it a lovely morning! Now, I'm sorry to have to upset you on such a fine day, but I have sad news. The Reverend Simon Essery is no longer with us. We had such short notice there was no time to find someone to take over the service. So we thought we'd just sing some hymns together. And maybe a couple of old-time gospel tunes. Would everyone who is able please stay for Fellowship Hour following the service when we'll discuss this unfortunate situation."

In the stunned silence that followed, he went back to the organ and struck the opening notes of *'All the way my Saviour leads me.'*

CeeCee'd been suffering for over a week from a miserable summer cold, the kind that are so hard to shake, so Dottie had had to go to church on her own that day. As soon as she got home, she burst into the living room to tell CeeCee the latest news.

"He's gone! The reverend's gone! An' not a soul knows where in tarnation he's at!" Dottie threw herself down on the old rocker and began rocking as hard as she could. "Oh 'tis a real mystery, 'tis!"

CeeCee looked up in surprise from the book she'd been reading and said, "Is this for real, Dottie? Or are you having me on? Come on now …"

" 'Tis true, 'tis true! I swear on a stack a bibles! Dix tole us in the hall after the service. Oh he left a note awright. But all it said was he couldn't go on without her, meanin' Bertie of course, an' …"

"You don't suppose! No! That's impossible!"

"I know what yer thinkin'. That he might a done somethin' ta hisself." Dottie stopped rocking and tugged at her skirt. "Oh, I gotta get outta these tight clothes," she said, standing up. "No, I don't think so. Note said he was gonna look for his wife an' he'd be back for their stuff."

Before returning to her book, CeeCee said, "Guess this means Syd and Gussie'll have to postpone their wedding plans. Bound and determined to get remarried at Saint Peeps. Too bad!"

A couple of days later, a large envelope marked 'LAB' arrived in the mail. Myrna was careful not to peek at the contents before putting it on Gussie's desk. The town constable had come into the office late that morning. She'd made a quick trip over to the parsonage to see if there was any sign the Reverend Essery might have come back. Mostly a waste of time, as it turned out. A cube van was blocking the driveway and two men were loading boxes and bags into it. When she showed them her badge and asked to see their order form, it proved to be a shipping invoice to a storage warehouse. No name or telephone number on it. And no, the men said sorry but they had no idea whose goods they were packing. They were following orders from the boss of *We Store All* in the City. Name of Canning.

Making a mental note to check out this Canning fellow, she thanked them and walked across to the church office to see if Daffy knew what was going on. The church secretary was on the phone and excused herself long enough to say that yes, she'd let the moving men into the parsonage after a phone call from the reverend and no, she had no idea where he was calling from, he'd refused to say. She promised to contact Gussie later that day and went back to her caller.

Gussie was in the middle of opening the LAB envelope when her phone rang. It was Syd, sounding breathless.

"Hey Gus! Guess what! I got a line on the old guy! Woke up in the middle of the night and the name Jazzer popped into my head! You know how that can happen."

"Sure do. Thanks for not calling me *then*!" Gussie said, suppressing a chuckle.

"Yeah, I didn't think you'd appreciate it if I did. Anyway, and then I remembered the old guy from up to Slackerville was Jasper Cuttlecombe, only Dad always called him Jazzer."

"At last!" Gussie replied, dropping the envelope. Whatever was in it could wait, even if it did come from the lab. "Where is he?"

"You'll never guess! Over to Dunhampton! That retirement place, Our Happy Home! Pick you up in five!" He hung up before she had a chance to say anything.

40
MR. CUTTLECOMBE TELLS A STORY

Their interview with Jasper Cuttlecombe proved to be intriguing. If a bit unsettling. They had no trouble accessing his room. The cheerful receptionist was the same one who'd been behind the desk when Gussie had come over to visit old Eliza Roxton after the Denton murder, looking for information. The woman said she was sure Mr. Cuttlecombe would be delighted to see them. After they'd signed in, she told them to go up to the top floor and turn left. The room they were looking for was down at the far end facing the garden.

The receptionist was right. The old man was overjoyed to see them. He wasn't put off by Gussie's uniform as Mrs. Roxton had been. Said he hadn't had a visitor in 'a month a Sundays'. Said most folks he knew had long since passed on. He was a small man with a sparse salt and pepper moustache, the few wisps of matching hair on the top of his head neatly combed over to one side. Dressed in a comfortable grey-mix sweatsuit, he was sitting in a wheelchair by the window of his cramped little room and motioned to them to take a seat on the bed.

"No room for chairs in this here place. Only seat's this here contraption," he said, smiling a lopsided smile and slapping the arm of his chair. "An' do call me Jasper. What can I do for you?"

"Well, Mr. Cuttlecombe …" Gussie began, but was silenced by the old fellow who held up a finger.

"What did I just tell you? It's Jasper! Don't answer to that other fancy moniker. Never did me no good. Not a soul could spell it even."

"Okay, sorry," Gussie began again, but was interrupted by Syd who moved over closer to the old man.

"Hey, remember me? Dave Spilsbury's son? The *Bickerton Bugler*? Remember? He used to call you Jazzer?"

The old man reached for his glasses. Taking a well-worn handkerchief out of his sleeve, he gave the lenses a good polish before perching them on his nose. His watery blue eyes brightened as he peered closely at Syd.

"Hate wearin' these here cheaters. Make me look old," he said. "Davey's son? By jiminy, you're right! Hain't seen you since you was a little gaffer. How's Davey these days? You look just like 'im."

Syd hastened to tell the old man his father was one of those who had passed on.

"Real sorry to hear it, boy," he said. "Your pa was real good to me, aye, that he was. We useta chew the fat over a pot a coffee. Down at Jimmie's, you know. The variety store in Bickerton? That is, when he had the time. Allus busy on that paper, he was. So, why're you here?"

Gussie picked up the thread. "Jasper, we understand you used to live up real close to Slackerville. We're looking to find out what happened to the Slacker family, I mean, the Slacker family. Can you tell us anything about them?"

Removing his glasses and laying them back on the windowsill, the old man sighed and leaned back in his chair.

"Oh yeah, them Slackers. Whadda you wanna know? An' - why do you wanna know it?"

Gussie looked over at Syd. "Can't hurt to tell him, can it?"

Jasper's hearing was sharper than they thought. "Can't hurt to tell me what?" was his next question. "Me pins may be useless, but there sure ain't nothin' wrong with me hearin'," he said, looking down at his legs.

Gussie was beginning to think she was losing control of the situation. Here was the old guy asking the questions instead of them. Struggling to reassert herself, she told him about the property and what she'd found up there.

"You don't say!" was Jasper's response. "So *that's* what …" He stopped in midsentence and cleared his throat. "Well, now, you better get ready to set awhile. I gotta think on this a minnit." He cleared his throat and spat into his handkerchief.

"Can I get you something to drink, Jasper? Would you like a glass of water, I mean, a glass of water?" Gussie said, trying to be helpful. The old guy was right about one thing. The rate they were going, they could be here the rest of the day.

"Water? Never touch the stuff. Got me a secret stash a somethin' worth drinkin'." He winked. "Syd, me lad, reach under the bed, will you?" He chuckled as Syd squatted down and felt around for minute. "This it?" he said as he dragged a long flat box out from its hiding place. On the cover of the box was a large snowy picture. Across the top were the words 'Lovely Winter Scene – 1,000 pieces'.

"Hah!" Jasper said. "Figured no one would think on lookin' in there. Open it, boy, would you? Go ahead, open it!"

Syd did so and was surprised to find an array of those little bottles of alcohol that are served on airplanes. "Where on earth …?"

"Hah!" Jasper said again. "Got this here young ladyfriend what gets 'em for me. Don't know how. Don't wanna know. Alls I care about is I got 'em. Go ahead. Help yourselves."

Gussie wondered to herself if alcohol was allowed in the Our Happy Home. Deciding not to say anything, she said no thank you, she couldn't drink on duty, but Syd was welcome to, if he wanted. After carefully lifting the box up beside him on the bed, Syd looked at the bottles again. "What'll it be, oldtimer? Name your poison."

"Aw, whichever you come to first. I don't mind," Jasper said, stretching out his hand.

Gussie realized this was yet another delaying tactic. *Pretty crafty for an old geezer.* She waited until the contents of one small bottle each had been chugged down by the two men. "Okay now, Jasper, what can you tell us about Slackerville?"

"Quite a bit," the old fellow said, wiping his mouth with his sleeve. "Well, lessee now. Them Slackers was real nice family. That is, the old Slackers. Didja know their great grandpa was one a the first white men to settle up there? Yessirree. He come over from the Old Country with his wife an' kiddies an' four or five cousin an' brother Slackers an' their families. Ended up there was so many of 'em, they called the place Slackerville. Useta be a real big settlement onct upon a time. Pass me another a them little bottles, will you Syd? Talkin' sure do make a man thirsty."

After a second bottle had been emptied, he continued, "Yep. A real cryin' shame what happened to them Slackers. Lotsa 'em left an' went Out West, lookin' for better farmin' land, you know. Them what stayed put up there didn't do so good. The old folks I useta know got sick with some kinda flu one hard winter an' died. By then, there wasn't near so many of 'em, what with drownins an' sickness an', well you know how it was back in them days. You say your pa is dead. What did he die of?"

Oh boy, another delay! Aloud Gussie said, "Syd could come back another time and visit you, Jasper. He can tell you all about it then, I mean, all about it." She glanced at Syd who picked up the ball and said, "Sure thing. I can do that. Be glad to."

Gussie went back to asking the questions and asked, "Well, how come there's no one living up there any more? At Slackerville, I mean. The road was barred off. The only place left is the old farm. It's been standing there vacant, I mean, vacant. For years, looks like. Didn't the Slackers have any children?"

"Sure as shootin' they did. A heap of 'em. The girls, I mind there was three of 'em, the girls got themselves married to fellas they met dancin'. At the Legion Hall over by Shankstown. Never came back home, as I recall. Not even to visit their own kinfolk." Jasper scrunched around in his chair and raised his arms over his head a couple of times. "Gotta keep movin' what I still can move, eh? Else I'll end up in th'infirmary. Any road, that's what the fella says what comes in to do them exercises with us." He dropped his arms.

"Did they have any boys?" Syd asked, trying hard not to look in the direction of the box of bottles. This wasn't a good time to drink any more booze now, was it? "What happened to the boys, Jasper?"

"There was three of 'em too, just like the girls. One got drownded in the crick when he were tryin' to get acrost it one winter. Fell through the ice. One was kilt in a car smash. It were the last one what went real bad. Eldon, now, that were his name. Donny, they called 'im. Baby a the bunch. Real good lookin' fella. Married Beulah Skinner right afore he went off to the War. She were a looker too. Yessir, got married an' shipped out a coupla nights later. Could be married life didn't suit 'im. Know it sure didn't suit me."

Gussie wasn't going to let anything else distract her. "So what happened after the War, I mean, after the War? Did he make it back home or …?"

"Oh yeah, he made it home awright 'n that's when all the trouble started. He were never the same when he come back. Real sad it were. Shell shock, they said. Got this idea the world were agin 'im. An' so he started in to shut the world out. Wouldn't let Beulah leave the place. Got her pregnant right away an' as soon as that one were born, he got her pregnant again. Don't know for sure how many kiddies she ended up with. Some of 'em mighta died. Anyways, Donny wouldn't let nothin' er no one near the place. Got hisself a coupla big dogs an' kep his guns handy. They say he brung a coupla weapons back from the War. Illegal like. Anyone dared come near the place, Donny sicced them ugly brutes of hounds on 'em an' showed up with a rifle or some such. Scared 'em off."

Syd and Gussie had the same thought. "Why couldn't …" Syd began, but Gussie broke in.

"Yes, why couldn't the police do anything about it? That was a dangerous situation, wasn't it? An accident waiting to happen, I mean, waiting to happen."

"You gotta think on how far away Slackerville was, back in them days. Not an easy place to get to. Road up an' in was two tracks, fulla holes. Where there *were* a road. Yep. Old Constable Gerald's father were the cop back then. Constable, uh, whatshisname, uh, wait a minnit, it's comin' back to me. Oh yeah, Eddie. Or was it Freddie? Doesn't make no never mind." He yawned and stretched out his hand. "Like I said, thirsty work this talkin'. An' rememberin'."

Syd passed over another bottle, and after a look from Gussie, slid the box back into its place under the bed.

"Yep. Old Constable uh, Eddie, that's it, Eddie! Tried to get in there one day. Was he sorry! Got the backside a his pants tore off. Scared the bejesus outta 'im. Any-the-hoo, Donny just got worse an' worse. Him an' his family was th' only ones left on the farm. We was all too scared even to go past the place. Never saw hide nor hair of 'em. Not outside er in town. After a while, we kinda forgot about 'em. The other folks moved away, but I stayed on. Till I hadda go away for a stretch. Then I had me accident an' hadda come here. Been here ever since. Didja wanna hear how I hurt me pins?"

Wonder how he pays for this place. Can't be cheap, that's for sure was going through Syd's mind when the old man suddenly stopped talking and closed his eyes. He had a pretty good idea of how, but guessed he'd better not say anything and wait until they were out of there. Gussie glanced at her watch and figured they'd gotten enough for now. She stood up. "Syd," she whispered. "I think we'd better leave. Jasper's getting tired." They started moving towards the door when Jasper's eyes popped open. "Bye now, Missus. Be sure you come back now, young fella. We can jaw some more. Sleepy now," and he yawned and closed his eyes again.

Gussie was beginning to get a glimmer of what had happened up at the old farm. What she imagined was too horrible to think about. *Better scoot back to the station and take a gander at those lab reports.*

41
NOT MUCH TO GO ON, BUT ...

On the way back to Bickerton, for a while there was silence in the front seat of the old truck. Then Syd and Gussie starting talking at the same time.

"Do you think ..." Syd said as Gussie broke in with "Got an idea ..." They started to laugh and Gussie said, "Let's start again. I think I've got a pretty good idea about what went on with the Slackers, I mean, with the Slackers. Come over to the station later on, will you? I'll give you a call first. I've just got to get busy and take a look at that package from the lab."

"Okeydokey, Gus. Sure thing," Syd replied, "I just remembered something. I figure the old guy must have made his money out of hooch. Dad used to keep a big brown bottle of something tucked away in behind an old machine in the pressroom. I saw it one time after Jasper had been there. I came in when Dad wasn't expecting me. He looked kinda sheepish and put his finger to his lips. I guess that's why he hooked up with Jasper. He must have liked a nip or two himself."

"You mean Jasper was making the stuff? I never heard anything about it. You know? I'll just bet he got caught. That's what he meant by 'a stretch'. The old guy did some time, I mean, did some time. I know there's been rumours that some folks are still doing it. Making hooch, I mean. Old Constable Gerald was never able to catch anyone at it. I remember Dad saying it was throwback to the rum-running days, I mean, to the rum-running days. You know, out across the Lake?" Gussie wrinkled her nose. "I don't know why anyone would want to drink that stuff. They could get poisoned. But I guess old habits die hard, I mean, die hard. Especially in some remote parts of the county."

"Yeah," Syd agreed. "There's still lots of dead end roads. Could be anything going on up past them and no one would know."

When Gussie broke open the seal on the envelope, she was disappointed to read the report that fell out on her desk. So far the findings were inconclusive, it read, but according to the bone specialist, the fragments from the boneyard had been badly gnawed by animals. They appeared to be from the body of a man in his thirties who had suffered some kind of trauma that was likely the cause of his death. It was a pity the skull was missing. It might have given an idea of what sort of trauma it was. From their condition, it would appear the bones had been lying in the depression under the fallen trees for quite a long time, maybe as long as twenty-five years.

The bones Gussie found on the front seat of the Jeep were those of a large canine. The poor animal must have starved to death. The leg bones had been chewed through. The bones from the well had been retrieved after the doctor put a rush order on them. They were still being examined, but as far as the specialists had been able to determine, they came from one adult, and two children. Children in their late teens from the condition of the teeth in the two smaller skulls. Those teeth had never known a dentist's drill. The bones had been underwater for some time and taken a lot of cleaning to get rid of the growth of some kind of algae attached firmly to the surfaces.

Gussie shuddered when she read that. *Must have been why the water was so green.* According to the attached letter, another report would be following soon. Maybe in a few months. The lab was really backed up and had to concentrate on more recent cases. *Doesn't tell me all I want to know, but maybe that's all I'm going to find out. If what I think happened is what really happened, well, I can't spend any more time on it. The main thing now is to clean up the place so Mr. Kibbidge feels safe to go up there again. I think the time we spent on the case was worthwhile. For that reason alone. If nothing else.* Or so she justified to herself. She picked up the phone to call Syd.

42
KILLING BLUE DEVILS

Syd and Gussie were sitting in her office at the police station, phone calls suspended, interruptions discouraged. Syd had brought them each a coffee from Jimmie's and a couple of muffins from the Cosy Corner. It was getting late, but they decided to delay eating dinner until after they'd had a chance to talk. That is, if nothing startling happened in the meantime. Myrna had been sent home, as Jordy, the night man, was due in shortly. And Wednesday was usually a quiet night.

After the muffins had been polished off, and the coffee had cooled enough to drink, Gussie showed Syd the report from the lab. He agreed with her it sure wasn't very conclusive. They would have to wait until they heard more to be certain. Gussie sipped at her coffee reflectively.

"Well anyway, this is what I think, Syd. I think it could have happened this way. For some reason we'll never know, Eldon Slacker decides to leave the farm. Either he's had enough of being cooped up there, or enough of family life, or he's going through a really crazy spell, I mean, a real crazy spell. If it was true he'd been shell-shocked during the War, he might have done crazy things. Anyway, he decides to leave. But there's no way he's taking the family with him. They might just let it slip to someone that he's been keeping them prisoner all those years. So he decides to go it alone. This means getting rid of them, I mean, getting rid of them. So he kills his wife and children and dumps them in the well. So they can't be found in case anyone came looking." She stopped to take another sip of coffee.

"That's the reason for the rocks and the heavy cover and the bars. He blocks the road in too. He thinks he's got it all planned out for his escape, I mean, his escape. But Mother Nature intervenes. Sure, he has the old Jeep stashed in that shed up in the woods where he puts his last remaining dog. And a box of clothes and other stuff. But on his way up to the Jeep for the last time, a sudden storm comes up and catches him."

"Yeah," Syd interjected. "After we saw there'd been a blow-down, I checked with the weather department and sure enough. A 'localized tornado' they called it. Went through about that time. I guess no one thought to check on the family as they'd been pretty well forgotten. If you believe old Jasper."

"So, in the blow-down," Gussie continued, "Eldon gets hit on the head by one of those big heavy pines, I mean, one of those pines. And gets trapped under it. And dies. The poor dog is stranded in the Jeep, and starts to gnaw at itself when it's driven mad with hunger." Gussie felt sick at the idea.

"And it's not till Rab Kibbidge comes along and buys the place that all this stuff comes to light. How did he find out about the old farm anyway?" Syd wondered.

"That's a bit of a mystery in itself. CeeCee Denton told me a strange lady came into the shop one day and they got to talking about farming. She's the one who told him about it, I mean, told him about it. Name's Emmalina Oates. The family used to be big here. Once upon a time. I asked around and it turns out they left town years ago, I mean, years ago. Something to do with the bank and a money scandal. Why she came back, no one seems to know."

"Oates, you said? If it's Oates, I think there was a Skinner in the family background. Lots of Skinners around here. Maybe one of them secretly helped out Beulah Skinner that was. How else would the Slackers've managed up there for so long with just the food they could grow themselves? What about all the other stuff you need on a farm? Or in the house? Or anywhere else?"

"Yeah, I wondered about that myself."

"I can see the headline now. **SLAUGHTER UP AT SLACKERVILLE.**"

"Oh no! You can't write that! Everyone and his cousin will be traipsing up to see where it all happened and bothering poor Mr. Kibbidge."

"They'd be lucky to find it on a map!" Syd said and they both laughed.

"Well, it doesn't look like we can do any more tonight, does it? Let's get out of here!" he said, taking Gussie by the hand. "Hey, did I tell you? I think I found us a place to live!"

Rab and Aaron stood at the edge of what was once a sea of blue. No longer. On the way up, they thought they smelled smoke, but it had been raining off and on so they weren't sure where it was coming from. Aaron had come up to cut down the Blue Devils and plow under what was left. It was too late for a crop this year, he said, but after it was plowed, Rab could sow a crop of winter wheat, turn that under in the spring and start fresh. Rab was so glad to have the well cleared that he didn't care about losing a year.

As soon as they'd driven into the property, they could see something was missing. Where the old farm house had been was a heap of smoking ruins. Most of it had fallen through into the cellar below. With a southwest wind driving it, the fire had spread into the field of Blue Devils and burned them to the ground. All those old dry weeds must have helped.

"Musta bin hit by lightning," Aaron said, pulling out a pack of cigarettes and searching in his pocket for a match. "Yeah, that coulda bin it. We had a bit of a storm last night, kept us awake. Musta bin up here too. What about your place?"

Rab was so dumbfounded at the sight in front of him, he didn't answer right away. He kicked at the blackened ground a couple of times. "Yep. Guess so. Yep. Some bad storm at our place too."

"Well, could be it's all to the good," Aaron said. "The fire's got rid of the Blue Devils. Could be as the bad luck got burned up with them."

"Sure hope so," said Rab.

POSTSCRIPT

> Albert and Katrina (née Bergner) Woodcock and big brother Jesse are thrilled to announce the arrival of twins Royal (5 lbs 2 oz) and Regina (4 lbs 4 oz) on September 5th, 1974 at Dunhampton General Hospital.

About the Author

Now retired from the hectic world of advertising copywriting, Laura Haferkorn is living on the North Shore of Lake Ontario with her husband, Canute, and two Dandie Dinmont terriers. Keenly interested in local history wherever she lives, and an observer of life in the country and in small towns, she is working on her third book in the Gussie Spilsbury series. Her other writings can be found at her website: www.laura-haferkorn.com.

CPSIA information can be obtained at www.ICGtesting.com
Printed in the USA
LVOW07s0140270914

406096LV00001B/12/P

9 781460 245712